Copyright © [2024] by [Ashley Henderson

Ashley Henderson
ashleypublishing2024@gmail.com

HitWorld Legends Never Fold

by Ashley Henderson

Chapter 1

Saint Paul was like a storm you couldn't escape from. The streets were rough, raw, lined with graffiti covered buildings and cracked sidewalks that told a thousand stories. Only the strong thrived here, and the smarter ones ruled. In this world, HitWorld ran the game. They weren't just some hustler. They were the ones everyone in the city either feared or respected. HitWorld was tight, and in Saint Paul, that meant everything. HitWorld's spots were Sunray, Old Hudson Road, and Westminster all marked out by

their crew. If you weren't HitWorld, you had no business here.

Rolling down old Hudson rd in a midnight blue Chevy Bubba with deep tinted windows, . People scattered as they passed, heads down, but eyes peeked from under hoodies, watching them and the ride. The car's engine growled low, a beast prowling through familiar territory.

Next to him was Ready, his right-hand man. There weren't any bosses in HitWorld, nobody took orders. It was loyalty first and the streets second. Every one of them can hold their own and would stand on business for any of the brothers. When they said they were all they had, they meant it. And right now, they were all on high alert. Pulling up in the sunray parking lot

Ready leaned back in his seat, eyes scanning the street.

"Yo, Hit, somethin' doesn't feel right tonight. Got that itch, you feel me?"

Hit gave a small nod, his gaze fixed ahead. "Yeah, streets feel different. People actin' funny, like they know somethin' we don't." He paused, fingers drumming on the wheel. "Keep your eyes peeled."

Ready kept his hands tucked in his jacket pockets, fingers wrapped around the handle of his piece, just in case. "Man, look at these fools," he muttered, eyeing a couple of young niggas standing by the wall, talking in low tones and side-eyeing the Chevy. "They actin' bold today."

"Wild Boy," Hit called, nodding at him.

Wild Boy grinned, flashing a set of gold teeth. "Ready. Streets talkin' real loud today."

Ready arched an eyebrow. "Yeah? What they sayin'?"

Wild Boy shrugged, his grin fading. "Somebody new in town. Real low-key but with money to burn. Word is he ain't just passin' through."

Hit's eyes narrowed. "Someone tryin' to step on our blocc?"

"Looks that way," Wild Boy said. "Ain't nobody got a name yet, but they makin' noise. People's heads turnin'."

Hit exchanged a look with Ready. He didn't like surprises, and he damn sure didn't like nobody moving in on the city. Whoever this was, he'd better be smart enough to keep his distance. But if not… Well, Hit was never one to shy away from a little gun play.

Wild Boy nodded and went back into the shadows. Ready glanced at Hit, his jaw set. "What's the move, Hit?

They slid back into the Chevy, Ready pulling out a fresh pack of Backwoods. He tore it open, took out a leaf, and started breaking down the weed, his fingers moving fast and practiced.

Ready sparked up, the thick, sweet smoke filling the car. He took a hit, letting the smoke linger in his lungs before exhaling slowly, watching it curl up toward the car's ceiling. "Calm always comes before the storm. Saint Paul's got too many players for it to stay quiet."

They passed the blunt back and forth, the Chevy filling with that haze, tension loosening but the edge never really gone. Hit's mind stayed sharp.

Ready exhaled a cloud of smoke, watching it dissipate. "You think these new niggas got the balls to make a move?"

"If they do, they're a damn fool," Hit muttered, taking another drag, his voice low. "I'm all for competition, but these young niggas? They think it's a game till they end up on a shirt."

The blunt was down to the last few hits when everyone started pulling up. Ready girl, Kaliyah, stood back, but her sharp eyes were scanning the lot, watchin' everyone. Kaliyah was as tough as they came. She didn't play about Ready or the crew. Hit nodded to Ready, the kind of nod that didn't need words. They both knew what was up.

    Rome had a steady grip on a metal pipe, his eyes lit with a readiness to protect what was his. "What's the word," he said, his voice hard. He was always ready for whatever , and he'd make sure nobody got away with messin' with HitWorld. His girl, Honey, leaned into him, all smiles, actin' like she was down for it too. But Honey was slick. What Rome didn't know was that she had her own side hustle going . Honey wasn't just out here to play nice; she was in it for herself, and her loyalty only ran as deep as her pockets.

Next to Honey were her girls Juicy and Kiki, two more names Thomas Hitta had in their pocket. They were all too happy to play along, acting like they were with Hit World, but the second money flashed from the other side, they were ready to sing.

Lyric, Hit's girl, stood close to him, keepin' her gaze hard on Honey and her friends. Lyric didn't like the way Honey was always smiling a little too sweetly. She'd noticed how Juicy and Kiki always looked like they had a secret. Lyric were solid for Hit and for the crew. If Honey and her friends were playing games, Lyric was gonna be the one to catch 'em.

Bone was the strong, silent one, standing back but ready to jump in if things went sideways. He didn't need to talk; his presence was enough. When Bone moved, everybody listened. Shoota was right by his side, a smile on his face but his eyes were cold. Shoota was the type who laughed through the fight; he enjoyed the rush. He glanced over at Ready, and they shared a nod.

Hit cleared his throat, getting everyone's attention. "Wild boy said it's some new niggas in town with money to burn we need to see who these new niggas is we already have a problem with them university niggas his voice low but dead serious.

Ready chuckled, taking a slow drag on the blunt. "Damn right," he said, letting the smoke curl from his lips. "Ain't nobody takin' ova our streets. We put too much work in."

Rome smirked, giving the pipe a quick tap against his hand.

Honey played her part well, noddin' like she was just as loyal as the rest of 'em. "They don't know what they're up against," she said, her voice sugary sweet.

Bone was the strong, silent one, standing back but ready to jump in if things went sideways. He didn't need to talk; his presence was enough. When Bone moved, everybody listened. Shoota was right by his side, a smile on his face but his eyes were cold. Shoota was the type who laughed through the fight; he enjoyed the rush. He glanced over at Ready, and they shared a nod.

Hit cleared his throat, getting everyone's attention. "Wild boy said it's some new niggas in town with money to burn we need to see who these new niggas is we already have a problem with them university niggas his voice low but dead serious.

Ready chuckled, taking a slow drag on the blunt. "Damn right," he said, letting the smoke curl from his lips. "Ain't nobody takin' ova our streets. We put too much work in."

Rome smirked, giving the pipe a quick tap against his hand.

Honey played her part well, noddin' like she was just as loyal as the rest of 'em. "They don't know what they're up against," she said, her voice sugary sweet.

But inside, she was already planning her next move, making sure she stayed in the loop. Her friends Juicy and Kiki exchanged a quick look behind her, knowing they were all in on the same game.

Kaliyah leaned over to Lyric, keeping her voice low. "I don't trust her," she murmured, eyeing Honey. "She's always actin' like she's here for Rome, but I've seen her makin' moves that don't add up."

Lyric nodded, watching Honey closely. "Me neither. I'm gonna keep an eye on her."

They might have been standing as a crew, but Lyric knew how to read people, and Honey didn't sit right with her. She'd been around enough to spot a fake.

Bone stepped forward, a steady presence, his gaze fixed on the ground like he was picturing what he'd do to anyone who crossed them. "Ain't no one steppin' on our blocc," he said, his voice a deep rumble.

Shoota laughed, his eyes glinting in the dark. "They gon' regret even lookin' this way."

Ready, as solid as a rock, was bouncing on his feet, like he couldn't wait to get out there. "I was ready for this. We gon' show 'em what HitWorld's about."

When they finally split up, Honey pulled Juicy and Kiki aside. "Y'all know what to do," she whispered, her voice low and secretive. "We gon' get paid, as long as we keep 'em fed."

Juicy grinned, nodding. "As long as they don't catch on, we are good."

Kiki smirked. "HitWorld thinks we're down for 'em, but we just playin' the game."

From the shadows, Lyric watched the three of them, suspicion growing in her gut. She didn't trust them one bit. Whatever they were up to, she'd find out, and when she did, she'd make sure they knew what it meant to betray Hit World.

Hit and Ready rolled up to the spot, the familiar warehouse on the east side of Saint Paul. The building was weathered, with broken windows and graffiti splashed across the brick, but inside it was all business HitWorld's home base.

As they stepped inside, four figures were already waiting.

"Yo, fellas," Ready called, giving a two-fingered salute.

Hit nodded to the crew. We need to figure out who these new niggas are.

Wild Boy let out a sharp laugh, gold teeth flashing. "Let me find out who it is, Hit. I'll make them disappear, real quiet-like."

Bone, his voice low and rough. "Ain't nobody takin' the east side from us."

Rome leaned forward, voice smooth and steady. "Before we make any moves, we need intel. We don't know who these niggas is, where they came from, or what they want. That's where we start."

Shoota sat listening to everyone talk rolling up a backwood.

The crew nodded, each of them ready to play their part. But as they started to move, Hit caught sight of a familiar face lingering by the doorway to Rome's girl,

Honey. She was a fixture around their crew, always around when Rome was, her presence both comforting and, sometimes, suspect. Honey was loyal on the surface, but Hit had always sensed something else, a look in her eye that didn't sit right.

Chapter 2

"Yo honey," Hit called voice sharp where your girls at.

Honey sauntered over, a sly smile on her lips. " out handling' business but I got y'all back Hit

"Do you?" Ready cut in, his tone a little sharper.

honey's eyes flashed just a little too quick. "I'm here, aren't I? She gave Hit a lingering look, but he wasn't buying it,

HitWorld knew the heat was on. It was just a matter of time before shit popped off.

Hit, Ready, and Rome posted up on Old Hudson, eyes scanning every corner.

The crew was tight, but the weight of what was coming made everyone a little more tense. Lyric stood next to Hit, her expression sharp. Kaliyah stayed by Ready's side, eyeing the surroundings like she always did. Bone and Shoota were just a little farther down the block, keeping an eye on Westminster

Honey, Juicy, and Kiki rolled up like it was just another day, but Red didn't buy it. She could see Honey's fake-ass smile from a mile away. It wasn't just the way Honey strutted through the block—it was the way she was glued to Rome's side and the way she'd kept texting throughout the morning, barely paying attention to what was going on.

Red wasn't having it.

"You think you can just roll up here and act like you run this shit?" Red muttered under her breath, loud enough for Mocha and Lyric to hear. "Nah. She ain't foolin' nobody."

Mocha glanced at Red. "Don't start, Red. We need to keep our heads clear."

But Red was already locked on Honey, who was still acting like everything was cool. "She keeps texting like she got somethin' to hide. If she's got another life, I'm about to find it out."

Mocha sighed, trying to keep her calm. "We'll deal with it. Just—"

Before she could finish, a black Chevy pulled up slowly, its tinted windows dark enough to hide the face inside. Everyone on the block stopped what they were doing, eyes narrowing. The sound of the car's engine was like a signal, and within seconds, everyone in HitWorld was on alert.

Rome's hand went straight to his pipe, ready for whatever came next. He stood tall, his stance letting everyone know he wasn't afraid of whatever was about to happen. Bone and Shoota stepped into position, their eyes locked on the Chevy as it cruised by.

The car stopped in front of HitWorld's crew. The window rolled down, but the person inside didn't get out. Manny, a known hitter from university popped his head out, a smirk on his face.

"What's good, HitWorld?" Manny called out, his voice dripping with arrogance. "Y'all out here like you really run this place. Ain't nobody told y'all the streets got new owners?"

Ready stepped forward, his voice low and dangerous. "The only owner here is death, Manny. You and your boys better keep it movin'."

Manny laughed, but it was dry. "Oh, I'm movin', don't worry. Just lettin' y'all know—we got some business we need to handle. And some of your people already know what's comin'."

He glanced over at Honey, who was standing near Rome, texting once again. The shift in her stance was subtle, but Red saw it. Honey didn't make eye contact with Manny, but the tension between them was undeniable.

Red's eyes locked on Honey, her anger simmering. "You know him?" she called out, loud enough for everyone to hear.

Honey straightened up, not even acknowledging Red's question. But Red didn't care about her silence. "You think you can hide behind Rome, but you ain't foolin' nobody. I see that snake in you, bitch."

Honey's expression hardened. "Scared little bitch," she shot back, her voice dripping with venom.

Red didn't flinch. "You don't know who you fuckin' with, do you? You cross HitWorld, and I promise you, it's a wrap."

Honey moved forward like she was gonna do something, but before she could get too close, Red was already on her. Without warning, she shoved Honey back, sending her stumbling. "You don't get to talk to me like that, bitch," Red spat, her voice cutting through the air.

Rome stepped forward, trying to get in between them, but Red was on fire now. "Nah, fuck that. She needs to understand there's a price for playin' both sides. And I'm the one that's gonna make her pay."

"Red, chill," Mocha said, stepping in front of her. "This ain't the time."

But Red wasn't listening. "She gon' make the time, Mocha. I'm done with this snake."

By now, everyone in Hit World was stepping up, ready to back Red if shit hit the fan. Bone, Shoota, and Ready were all standing behind her, their eyes locked on Honey and the rest of the women, who seemed unsure about what to do next.

Rome stepped up, trying to push back a little, but his voice was low and steady. "Let her breathe, Red. We got bigger shit to deal with. Don't let this little drama fuck us up."

But Red didn't care. "Drama? This bitch ain't no drama, Rome. She's a liability. She's workin' both sides, and that's a problem for all of us."

Manny, still in the Chevy, laughed. "Yo, HitWorld's really out here acting like y'all got this on lock. We already made our move. time's up."

Hit stepped forward, his voice cold and commanding. "You tell your crew they better stay the fuck outta our way. Bodies about to start droppin' soon, and it won't be nice

You fucking with the wrong people. Manny, you've been warned, Ready said."

Manny just grinned, his smirk never fading. "We'll see, Hit. We'll see."

With that, the Chevy sped off, disappearing down the block. The tension didn't leave, though. It hung thick in the air, and everyone could feel it.

Lyric turned to Hit, her voice low. "We need to move fast. They're not just talkin' now—they're coming for us."

Hit nodded, his eyes narrowing. "Tomorrow. We bring the heat. No more games."

Red shot one last look at Honey, her words cold. "One more wrong move from you, and I'm head-shot that bitch. cross HitWorld, you gon' learn the hard way."

Honey stayed quiet, but Red had that look in her eyes. The game had just changed, and there was no turning back.

Chapter 3

The sun had barely risen over Old Hudson when HitWorld was already gathering on the block. This wasn't just any day; today, they were going to show who really ran things. Hit called the whole crew together, and you could see it in his eyes—he wasn't playing.

Bone, Ready, Rome, Shoota, and Wild Boy were lined up, each one armed and looking like they were ready for anything. The whole crew was feeling the pressure, and no one was about to back down. The energy was electric, each of them fueled by the disrespect Manny and

had shown.

Red and Mocha stood near the back with Lyric and Kaliyah, but even they were on edge. Red's eyes never left Honey, who was off to the side with Juicy and Kiki, pretending like she hadn't heard a word of the threats thrown her way yesterday.

As Hit looked around, he made sure to meet the gaze of every single member. He wanted them to understand just how serious this was. This wasn't just another day on the block—this was about respect, survival, and putting an end to little games.

"Alright, listen up," Hit started, his voice carrying through the morning air. " thinks they can us. They think they can move our territory like we ain't been holding it down for years. Today, we show 'em what happens when you with HitWorld."

A murmur of agreement ran through the crew. Each one of them was ready, their loyalty running deeper than words. It was more than just territory—it was family.

And they weren't about to let anybody

them.

"Ready, Rome, you take the northside of Old Hudson. Watch for anyone looking out of place," Hit instructed. "Bone, Shoota,

Wild Boy you're with me. We're gonna make a run to Sunray and make sure nobody's lurking around there."

Red leaned over to Mocha, her eyes flashing. "Watch Honey, Mocha. She makes one wrong move, and I'm on her."

Mocha shook her head but didn't argue. She could feel the tension building, and with poking at them, now wasn't the time for division within the crew. But she knew Red wasn't one to back down, especially when her gut was telling her something was wrong.

Honey must have sensed Red's glare because she finally looked up, meeting Red's eyes with a defiant stare. It was as if she was daring Red to say something.

"What's your problem, Red?" Honey sneered, her voice carrying just enough attitude to be heard. "You keep lookin' at me like I'm the enemy."

Red smirked, crossing her arms. "Maybe you are, Honey. All I know is I don't trust you. And trust is everything in Hit World."

Honey rolled her eyes, brushing her off. "You don't trust anybody, Red. That's your problem."

Red took a step forward, her voice low but laced with venom. "My problem is the snakes in the crew.

And if you keep messin' around, you might just find yourself dealt with."

Lyric stepped in, putting a hand on Red's shoulder to keep things from boiling over. "Let it go, Red. Today's about the block, not her."

Hit's voice broke through the tension, calling the crew back into focus. "Alright, we move out now. Everyone knows their spot. And remember—eyes open, ears sharper. Ain't nobody slippin' today."

The crew split up, each group heading in their assigned direction. Hit, Bone, and Shoota moved out toward Sunray, walking in formation, pipes ready in case anything went down. The streets were quiet for now, but that didn't mean they weren't being watched. Sunray was deep in HitWorld territory, but lately, had been creeping in closer than anyone was comfortable with.

"Yo, Hit," Bone muttered as they walked. "You really think they're gon' pull somethin' today?"

Hit didn't look back, his gaze focused ahead. "I don't think they got the balls to come at us head-on. But that doesn't mean they won't try somethin' sneaky."

Shoota nodded, glancing around. "We just gotta stay a step ahead. Show 'em they picked the wrong crew to mess with."

Meanwhile, on the north side of Old Hudson, Ready and Rome were holding it down, keeping a lookout for anything unusual. Rome was pacing, tapping against the pipe he kept close at all times. He was itching for action, and it was clear he wouldn't mind if tried to show up.

"Man, I hope they do pull up," Rome said, his voice tight with anticipation. "I'm tired of these fools thinking they can play games with us."

Ready smirked, shaking his head. "Careful what you wish for, bro. But if they do show up, best believe we ain't takin' no prisoners."

Back near the main block, Red and Mocha kept their eyes on Honey, who hadn't stopped whispering to Juicy and Kiki. Red was grinding her teeth, every word that left Honey's mouth making her want to snap.

Finally, Red had enough. She stepped forward, not caring who saw her or what they thought. "Yo, Honey," she called out, her tone daring her to respond. **"You got somethin' to say to the crew? 'Cause all that whisperin' ain't gon' cut it."**

Honey looked up, annoyance flashing in her eyes. **"Mind your business, Red."**

Red took another step, her voice dropping to a deadly whisper. **"You are my business, Honey. You are in HitWorld's territory, and you actin' like you don't know the rules. You cross us, and I swear, I'll make sure you regret it."**

Honey smirked, shaking her head like she wasn't fazed. "You ain't scarin' nobody, Red. You just mad 'cause I don't bow down to you."

Mocha moved in, putting a hand on Red's arm. "Enough. We got more important things to handle today. Manny and his crew, the enemy, remember?"

Red took a step back but kept her gaze on Honey. "We'll see. Just remember—you slip once, and you're done."

As the day wore on, each group held their ground, eyes scanning every corner, every shadow, watching for any signs of movement. Hours passed, and the sun began to dip lower in the sky, casting long shadows over the block.

Then, just as the crew started to regroup back on Old Hudson, a message came through on Lyric's phone. It was a text from an unknown number, but she recognized the warning instantly—it was from a source that was on the block . She showed it to Hit, her face tense.

"They're makin' a move tonight," she said. "Manny is planning to hit one of our spots on Westminster. They think we're playin."

Hit's jaw clenched, his face darkening. "Then we hit 'em back. Tonight."

Ready and Rome nodded, their expressions dead serious. The message was clear: tonight wasn't going to end quietly. They were going to show Manny and his crew that HitWorld has nothing to play with.

"Everybody meet up at Westminster," Hit commanded, his voice cold. "We're putting an end to this tonight."

The crew moved as one, the weight of their brotherhood unbreakable. The sun was nearly gone now, and darkness settled over the block, but HitWorld was ready. This was their hood, and no one was going to play in their face.

Chapter 4

The east side was always in motion, but tonight on Westminster it was alive. Hit, Ready, WildBoy,Shoota,and Bone were deep on the grind, working their hustle on every corner, and watching the street that was under their rule.Manny didn't show up that night but staying sharp, making money, and keeping the heat off their backs. Tonight was about holding their ground.

Hit these niggas ain't coming' Shoota said I'm about to go to the crib with my bitch.

Sound like a plan Wild boy said I'll meet up with y'all niggas tomorrow at the warehouse.

Hit make sure y'all bring them bags with y'all.

Aight im out Rome and Bone said.

Hit and Ready went they separate ways

The next day The spot was thick with smoke and the smell of cash. HitWorld had the place on lockdown, tables covered in stacks of bills, scales, and baggies. Each member of the crew was locked in. Wild boy who was always late wasn't there yet but everyone was focused, and running on that adrenaline only the hustle could bring. Hit was at the head, counting stacks with eyes sharp as ever. Ready leaned back, rolling a blunt, one eye on the door, the other on the cash.

"Real money movin' now," Ready said with a grin, sparking up. "Manny, think they're out here hustlin'? They have no clue what we bringin' in."

Rome's phone buzzed again, lighting up for the fifth time in ten minutes. Honey's name flashed across the screen. He frowned, shoving it back in his pocket without answering.

Ready chuckled, catching it. "Yo, Honey blowin' you up again? That girl doesn't know when to stop."

Rome smirked, shaking his head. "She gotta chill. Ain't nobody got time for her games, not when we sittin' on this kinda bread."

Hit's phone buzzed, and he picked it up, eyebrows raised. Lyric. Turning away from the table, he answered, "Yo, what's good, Lyric?"

Her voice came through the line, tense. "Hit, listen, some nigga's been lurkin' around the bar asking about y'all. They look like they are from another set, talkin' slick, sayin' they lookin' for HitWorld."

Hit's eyes narrowed. "Where do they say they are from?"

They didn't say but they didn't look local. Could be trouble. Hit."

These must be the new niggas Wild boy was talking' about.

Hit nodded. "Stay low. We'll slide through later and see what's good."

He hung up, looking around. "Yo, we got eyes on us. Some niggas sniffin' 'round the bar, askin' questions."

Wild Boy, who had just walked in and caught the tail end of the call, let out a low laugh. "More niggas they got a death wish or somethin' coming' round here lookin' for trouble. HitWorld don't just sit back and watch."

Wild boy about time you joined us Ready said givin' him the blunt

Wild boy flashed his gold teeth man a nigga had somethin' to take care of.

Hit shakin' his head I bet you did bitch you always dealin' with crazy hoes that's way.

"Naw that's Rome's problem Wild boy said my bitches know they place he start laughing'

Alright pussy ass nigga's Bone said cuttin' in let's introduce the new member to HitWorld.

Enoch, the newest member, leaned back, watching Wild Boy with interest. "Guess I'm in the right place then." He reached into his backpack, pulling out a stack and tossing it on the table. "Made some moves on the side. Thought I'd throw it in the pot."

The crew glanced at each other, nodding with approval. Bone leaned over, giving Enoch a nod. "You makin' yourself real at home, bro. We could use a solid head like yours 'round here."

Shoota leaned back, eyeing the pile of money. "More paper, more problems—but that's why we keep pipes close."

As if on cue, Rome reached under the table and brought out an old duffel, unzipping it to reveal more firepower. He laid a shiny new pistol on the table with a grin. "Just in case anybody tries to test us on this blocc."

Enoch looked over, impressed. "Y'all rollin' heavy, I see."

Hit picked up the pistol, giving it a quick once-over before putting it down. "Gotta be. Manny and his crew think they can step on our blocc? Nah. They take one step too far, and we send them back in body bags."

Mocha walked over, grabbing a few bundles off the table to bag them up. She shot Enoch a sideways glance, raising an eyebrow. "So, you really know Kiki, huh? Has she always been like that?"

Enoch laughed, shaking his head. "Man, Kiki has been a scandal since day one. She'll cozy up to anybody with a dollar, but don't trust her as far as you can throw her."

Red, who had been watching from the side, smirked, sliding a blade across a block of powder with precision. "We ain't got time for fake loyalty 'round here. Kiki's days are numbered if she keeps messin' around."

Enoch leaned back, nodding as he took it all in. "Guess we are all on the same page. Anybody steppin' out of line gets what's comin'."

Shoota grinned, loading his pistol with a click that echoed through the room. "That's why we all got pipes, right? In case somebody needs a reminder."

The air went still as they each checked their pieces, the clicks and clacks of metal filling the room. It was like an unspoken pact—loyalty was earned, and betrayal was a bullet with your name on it.

Hit went back to counting the cash, his gaze never wavering. "This stack here, that's from the last re-up. Ready, take it out to the back room and get it cleaned."

Ready nodded, gathering up the stacks and moving toward the back. "Easy. Money talkin' out here like we on a new level. Let Thomas Hitta's think they makin' noise. Ain't nothin' but whispers compared to this."

Rome caught Enoch's eye, tossing him a bundle. "Welcome to Hit World, E. You bring that heat, and we bring loyalty. Just know, any slip-ups and we handle business fast."

Enoch smirked, pocketing the bundle. "Don't need to tell me twice. Y'all keep it real, and I'll keep my head down. And if Kiki tries any games… trust, I'll be the first to set her straight."

Rome laughed, nodding with approval. "That's what I like to hear! We all got each other's backs here. Ain't no room for traitors."

They continued bagging up the product, counting stacks, and loading magazines, the sounds of their hustle filling the room. Every move was deliberate, every glance a reminder that loyalty was everything. They'd come too far to let anyone tear Hit World apart.

By the time they wrapped up, the place was locked down tight, every piece of cash counted, every bag sealed, every weapon loaded. The crew shared a look, each one of them knowing the weight they carried on their shoulders. They weren't just some crew out here hustling—they were HitWorld. Them bitch-ass niggas think they can mess with this blocc? They're dead wrong.

Chapter 5

The sun was starting to set over Westminster, casting an orange glow across the blocc. The quiet felt different this time—like a storm was brewing. They all knew it. The sound of money being bagged and guns being loaded didn't mean peace was coming. It meant war.

Hit sat in his car, parked on the side of the street, staring out at the blocc. His phone buzzed again, another call from Lyric. He answered quickly.

"Yo, Lyric, what's good?" Hit said, his voice low but with an edge of concern.

"Hit, there's more of 'em now. Those dudes from the bar, they're out here lurkin' heavy. I saw a couple of them pull up around the corner. I think they're lookin' to make a move on us."

Hit's grip on the steering wheel tightened. He could feel the weight of the situation in his bones. This was it. They were getting too bold.

"Alright, stay inside. Don't let nobody in the bar. I'm about to handle this."

Hit hung up and took a deep breath, looking out at the street again. There was no way he was gonna let Manny and his crew step foot on their blocc without paying for it. He knew they were hungry, but they didn't know what hungry was until they saw HitWorld in full force.

He turned the key in the ignition and pulled off, tires screeching as he hit the gas. Ready was the first call he made.

"Ready, what's up?"

"I'm already on it," Ready responded, sounding calm as always. "I got to call Rome, Enoch and Wild boy. We'll hit them from the east side, circle 'round 'em."

"Bet," Hit said, his eyes narrowing. "Don't get caught slippin'. We gotta make sure we hit 'em hard."

As he spoke, he glanced in the rearview mirror and saw Bone's car roll up behind him, his black Chevy keeping pace. Bone and Shoota had a look of focus on their face, no bullshit. The two cars were now cruising side by side, like they were on a mission. It was about to go down.

Back at the warehouse, Rome and Enoch were busy securing the place. The tension in the air was thick as they set up shop, counting money and bagging up work. The smell of fresh cut came from the tables in the back, and the sound of the vacuum-sealer bags closing echoed through the large space.

Rome pulled a stack of bills from his bag, counting it with precision. "Ain't no stoppin' this, Enoch. We got all the products we needed. Now it's time to make sure these boys on the other side know who runs this blocc."

Enoch didn't respond right away. He was too focused on checking the barrels of the guns in front of him, making sure everything was locked and loaded. His eyes flicked over to Rome.

"I've been watchin' these streets for a minute now. And Manny thinks they gonna walk in here like they own it. Ain't gonna happen."

Rome smirked as he slid a rubber band around the stacks of cash. "We need to send a message tonight. Let them know they fuckin' with the wrong crew."

Before Enoch could respond, his phone buzzed. He pulled it out and looked at the screen. It was a message from Ready.

"They're movin' in," Enoch muttered. "We ain't got much time."

Rome gave him a sharp look. "Let's go. We hit 'em fast, hit 'em hard. Ain't no second chances."

As the two of them moved toward the exit, the sound of a car pulling up outside could be heard. Wild Boy was already moving toward the back of the warehouse, setting up a lookout.

"Stay low," Rome said to Enoch. "When they moved to the back door Wild boy was standing there tf y'all got pipe pointin' to my head."

Rome bitch I ain't know that was you pullin' in Ready sent a text we need to meet them at the bar.

The three of them moved quickly, stepping out of the warehouse . Their eyes were focused, scanning the area as they walked toward the cars.

Ready had already rolled up, and now it was time to see who tf these niggas was.

Honey had been blowing up Rome's phone all damn day. Rome was done with the distractions, and as the crew geared up for war, his phone buzzed again.

"Fuck this bitch," Rome muttered, ignoring the call and tossing his phone onto the sea.

Lyric's voice crackled through Hit's phone as he was getting out the car

"Hit, where are you? There are more of 'em now. They've got backup.

"Alright, Lyric, I'm in the back, come open the door back here. We going to see what's to them now," Hit replied,

The cars sped down the Alley , the tension thicker now than ever everyone hopped out the car's

Hit's eyes narrowed. To the niggas outside This wasnt Manny and his crew These niggas weren't the same ones they'd seen hanging on the other side These niggas were different.

As they rolled up, Hit saw the distinct tattoos marking the crew—their faces hard as stone. Aye what's to you niggas Ready said why you lookin' for us Wild boy said after. The biggest nigga start walkin' up aye what's good my name Jace I'm not from here I ran shit in *Chicago my crew is the Chicago Kings*, a feared and respected crew from Chicago that had been known to drop bodies in the streets for years. They were ruthless, a crew with no mercy. These were the real hitters.

Rome's eyes widened. "The fuck? Do you niggas want."

"Enoch looked , his hand gripping his gun tighter.

Bone "Shit. We ain't got no time to waste.tf is it y'all lookin' for?"

"Let's talk," Jace said," Hit looked at them.

"We ain't here for war. Jace said

We didn't give a fuck if you was or wasn't lookin' for a war Shoota said.

Jace eyes cold as steel. He gave a slight nod of recognition to Ready, Rome, Enoch, and Bone, though it was clear they were all sizing each other up.

"Hit World?" Jace's voice was smooth but low. "Y'all the ones claimin' this blocc now?"

"We run this, " Hit responded, his voice calm but deadly.

Jace smiled a little, his expression still hard. "We ain't got no issues. Just makin' moves in the city, y'know? But we don't step on anybody's toes unless they ask for it."

There was a tense silence as the two crews stared each other down. The tension was thick in the air, but neither side pulled their guns yet. It wasn't the war they'd expected, but it was a standoff all the same.

After a moment, Jace spoke again, his voice a little softer but still filled with a certain weight. "But look, Hit… I ain't gonna lie to you. We been movin' product from Chicago to Saint Paul, and y'all been movin' some serious weight out here. I think we can make this work—get this money together. We run these streets back and forth, and no one can fuck with us."

Hit studied Jace for a moment, his mind working. The idea made sense. Teaming up could help them keep the whole region locked down—Saint Paul, Chicago, everywhere.

"Talk business, huh?" Hit muttered. "What's your play?"

"We move it all together. We're already good in Chicago, and we know how to push here. Let's combine forces and make these streets ours. We'll keep the money flowing, keep the enemies back, and we won't have to worry about Manny or his little crew."

Hit's eyes flicked over to his crew. He didn't make alliances easily, but something about Jace's confidence was making him consider it.

"We'll talk more," Hit said slowly, then turned to his crew. "For now, we watch. We see how they move."

Jace nodded. "Good We'll be in touch."

As the two crews stood there, a temporary truce was struck, but the streets still felt hot, like a fuse had been lit. HitWorld had just stepped into bigger waters, and the game was about to change for everyone.

Chapter 6

The warehouse on Third Street had always been a place of business. It was dark, grimy, and smelled like work. The only thing that made it stand out in the cold, desolate block was the crew that ran it—HitWorld. The crew didn't need much to feel at home; all they needed was their money, their product, and their loyalty to each other. This wasn't just another meeting; this was the decision that would change everything.

The usual people were gathered around: Hit, Ready, Wild Boy, Bone, Enoch, Shoota, Rome ass wasn't there yet. The place was set up with bags of cash on one table, bags of product on another, and a few loose firearms scattered across the room, just in case someone decided to make a move. HitWorld had been running things in their area, but the streets had a way of testing everyone who thought they were untouchable.

Hit walked in, boots hitting the concrete floor with a purpose. He didn't have to speak right away. His presence alone told everyone to shut the hell up. He didn't trust easily, but he trusted his crew. They had all made it this far together, and now it was time to talk business.

"So, what's the word?" Hit asked, looking around at his brothers. His voice was steady but low, the calm before the storm. He made his way to the center of the room, taking a seat at the table. The others followed suit, settling into the chairs around him. Everyone's eyes were on him, waiting for him to make the first move.

Enoch leaned back against the wall, his eyes never leaving Hit. "Jace's proposal ain't a small thing, Hit. We are talking about teaming up with the Chicago

Kings. That ain't some quick decision. We let 'em in, we might be opening doors we can't close."

Ready stood up and paced across the room, his arms crossed tightly. He had been thinking hard about this. "I hear you, Enoch. But think about it. We ain't just running the blocc anymore. We are talking about taking over states, maybe even the whole region. We could move weight across lines, make stacks we ain't even dreamed of."

Wild Boy took a long pull off his blunt, blowing out the smoke slowly. "I don't trust outta town niggas. We got our own thing going, why the fuck do we need

Chicago in the mix? Niggas come in, niggas take over. I'm good."

Bone nodded, rubbing his chin thoughtfully. He was always quiet, but when he spoke, people listened. "The money's good, but like Enoch said, we don't know what else comes with these Chicago niggas. We don't know what their beef is. They might bring heat from places we ain't even looking at."

There was a moment of silence. The weight of the decision hung in the air like a thick fog. Everyone knew that joining forces with the Chicago Kings meant more than just making money. It meant putting your trust in a whole new crew, one that didn't know the streets of HitWorld, one that didn't know the rules they lived by. But the money was tempting, and sometimes, the only thing that mattered in this game was how much you could stack before the streets swallowed you whole.

"I don't trust them either," Hit said, his voice cold. "But it ain't about trust. It's about power. We make this move, and we move like they do. They know the game, and they know the hustle. We ain't got the resources to move weight like they can, but if we join forces, we can run the whole area. Ain't no more playing small-time. We go big, or we don't go at all."

Sienna, one of WildBoy's hoe, came walking in the warehouse, her presence commanding attention as she strutted through the door, her heels clicking against the concrete floor. She had always known how to make an entrance, but right now, she was on edge. Her eyes scanned the room, and she could tell that the energy had shifted.

"Y'all niggas still talking?" she asked, her tone cool, but there was something underlying it—something that made the whole room stop and listen.

She wasn't part of the core crew, but Sienna always had a way of being in the mix. She wasn't shy, and she definitely wasn't afraid to speak her mind.

"I need to add something to the conversation," she continued, moving toward the table where Hit and the others were gathered. "I think we are all missing something big here." Her voice dropped, and everyone leaned in, sensing that something was about to go down.

She glanced around the room. "It ain't just about these Chicago Kings coming' in. It's about Manny and his crew. Those motherfuckers. Just teamed up with some niggas from Minneapolis.

The room went silent. The mention of Minneapolis made everyone's heads snap in her direction. Minneapolis had always been trouble, but teaming up with Manny? That was different. It wasn't just a local issue anymore—it was a problem.

"Hold on," Wild Boy muttered, his voice tense. "Bitch You telling me these niggas linked up with Minneapolis?

"Exactly," Sienna replied, her voice steady. "And They've been putting in work. Making alliances, talking trades, and they ain't about to stop."

"Shit," Ready cursed under his breath. "So now we got these niggas on both ends of us, and the Chicago Kings want to roll in too? What the fuck is going on in these streets?"

Hit stayed silent for a moment, his mind working fast. He wasn't surprised about Minneapolis making moves, but hearing about their partnership with Manny pussy ass hit harder than he expected. He had been expecting a fight, but this was different. They weren't just facing off against one rival gang anymore—they were facing an alliance.

Hit finally spoke, his tone dead serious. "But what they don't know is that HitWorld doesn't fold. Not now, not ever. We got heat, we got resources, and we got each other. Ain't nobody running us out of here. We handle this our way."

"Yeah, but we ain't gotta do this alone," Bone said. "If we roll with the Chicago Kings, we can take over everything. We can run Saint Paul and university. Hell, we can make our names known from Saint Paul to Minneapolis,to Chicago."

The room went quiet again. Every word that was said carried weight, and the decision wasn't easy. The streets didn't wait for anyone, and if they were gonna move, they had to move fast.

Enoch looked over at Shoota, who had been unusually quiet until now. Shoota rubbed his temple, thinking about all the angles. "Chicago Kings ain't no joke. We ain't here to play games with them. But ain't no way we're going down without a fight."

Then, just as everyone was getting lost in the weight of their words, Rome pushed through the door, his energy shifting the room's vibe. "Ayo, what the hell is going on here?"

Hit looked at him, eyes narrowing. "The streets are shifting, Rome. Manny and Minneapolis are comin' together for us, and we gotta decide whether we take them niggas Chicago Kings offer or we take the city by storm."

Rome let out a laugh, his voice sharp with street knowledge. "Shit I'm down for whatever we HitWorld either way we are going to win."

The room got tense again, the decision looming large. Hit stood up. "Alright, here's the play. We get in with the Chicago Kings, but we do it on our terms. We ain't nobody's sidekick. We run this. And ain't no one gonna take what's ours."

The crew nodded, the air charged with tension and anticipation. It was time to make their move.

Hit called Jace and told him to meet them at the warehouse.

Chapter 7

Still at the warehouse vibe today, was something' you could feel in the air. Everyone was still there—Hit, Ready, Rome, Bone, Wild Boy, Shoota, and Enoch—were all present. The place was buzzing with low conversation,waiting. No one was sure how this was gonna go, but the proposal from Jace and his crew couldn't be ignored. Either they played it right, or they could get left behind.

"Man, I don't trust this shit," Wild Boy muttered under his breath, scanning the area around the warehouse. His hand was resting on his piece, a nervous habit. "Ain't no way these out-of-town niggas gonna come in here like they run shit."

"Relax, Wild Boy," Ready said, his eyes narrowed but calm. "We ain't soft. Let's hear them out first. Jace might have the right idea. There's too much money on the table to not at least listen."

Hit, leaning against a pillar, stayed quiet for the moment. His expression was unreadable, as usual. He wasn't the type to jump into things without feeling it out first, but this was different. The game was changing, and sometimes, you had to adjust. If Jace and his crew could bring something to the table, then maybe it was worth it. But if it was just talk—then they'd find out soon enough.

"Yo, man. You good?" Rome asked, walking up to Hit. "You've been quiet."

"Yeah," Hit replied, his eyes scanning the room. "I'm just thinking. We gotta make moves, but we don't make moves blindly."

Before the conversation could go further, Sienna walked in with a quick step. Her eyes scanned the group, and she tossed a glance at Hit. "Yo, y'all better be ready. I got word the Chicago Kings are on their way. Jace and his people are serious about this. We either work with them, or we risk getting left behind."

Everyone in the room took a beat. The Chicago Kings were heavy hitters in the game. If Jace's proposal was real, it could mean a lot of money, muscle, and opportunity. But the question was, did they trust him?

Before anyone could speak up, the sound of a car door slamming outside broke the tension. The lookouts had radioed in that Jace and his crew had arrived. They were here.

A few minutes later, the front door of the warehouse creaked open, and in walked Jace and his crew. Tall, lean, with hard eyes and an air of confidence that said they weren't to be messed with. There were five of them in total, including Jace himself. Each one looked like they'd seen a battle or two, and they weren't scared of getting their hands dirty.

Jace walked up first, offering Hit a firm handshake. "We ain't got time to waste," he said, his voice low but serious. "We know what y'all doing out here, and we have the same goals. We have resources in Chicago that can help both our crews get rich, but we need to put aside the bullshit and get down to business."

Hit returned the handshake with a sharp, calculating look in his eyes. "I'm listening, Jace. But we don't trust nobody out here, not even our own sometimes."

Jace smiled, like he'd expected this reaction. "I get it. But you can't run the streets by yourself forever, man. This game's bigger than your block. We move the same way. You're in Saint Paul, I'm in Chicago. We can run the same game—drugs, money, guns—and move it up and down the Midwest. We got connections, muscle, and money. Y'all bring the experience and the hustle. Together, we make one hell of a team."

Ready stepped forward, his eyes still skeptical. "So what's in it for us? How do we know you ain't just trying to use us to get your hands on our blocc's?"

Jace didn't flinch. "We ain't trying to take over your blocc, man," he said, his voice steady but firm. "We trying to work together. Y'all heavy hitters, and so are we. So why not put us together to tear up Saint Paul and Chicago? You guys got the streets here, we got them out there. We built an empire. Move money. Stack. What's the downside?"

Bone, who hadn't spoken much yet, spoke up now. "How do we know we can trust you, though? You say we make money, but how do we make sure y'all ain't planning to pull some snake shit?"

Jace paused for a second before answering. "I'm not saying we can't make some mistakes along the way, but I'm not trying to waste time on games. I've got a network, and you've got muscle. We can keep each other in check. This is a partnership. We move together, or we die apart."

Shoota, who had been leaning against the wall, finally stepped up. His voice was calm but intense. "Alright, man. Let's say we agree. What's the first move? Where do we start?"

Jace motioned for one of his boys to open a suitcase. Inside was a set of papers—contracts, blueprints, the whole nine yards. "This here's the first step. We get everything in writing. This isn't just a handshake deal. I'm talking logistics, distribution, money, everything."

There was a slight pause before Sienna walked in from the back, her eyes scanning the room. "Yo," she said, speaking fast. "Tf do you want hoe WildBoy said.

I was about to let y'all know that Manny and Minneapolis about to roll up to one of y'all spot's but I can wait until after y'all down handling business call me Later Sienna said to WildBoy.

The room went dead silent for a moment. The tension had shifted, and everyone's mind went into overdrive.

Jace looked around the room, his eyes narrowing. "Well, now we know what we're really up against. The Thomas Hitta's? Let's deal with them, too. We handle business with you guys, and we can squash these bitches together."

Hit locked eyes with Jace. "Let's handle this. But know this: we don't fold."

Jace looked around the room, his eyes narrowing. "Well, now we know what we're really up against. Manny and his crew and Minneapolis ? Let's deal with them, too. We handle business with you guys, and we can squash these bitches together."

Hit locked eyes with Jace. "Let's handle this. But know this: we don't fold."

Chapter 8

The warehouse on Third Street was quiet for the moment, but it wouldn't last long. Hit ,Ready,WildBoy,Bone,Shoota,Rome and Enoch sat at the table with Jace and his crew, the papers spread out between them like a battlefield. The plans were laid out, thick blueprints outlining how to control the flow of money, drugs, and power between Saint Paul and Chicago. They went over the details again, the air tense, as the future of their partnership hung in the balance.

"Alright," Hit said, leaning over the table, tapping the papers with his finger. "Let's go over these numbers one more time. We clear on who gets what?"

Jace nodded, already knowing what was coming. He wasn't just here for the blueprint—he was here to seal a deal. "We ain't splitting fifty-fifty with Saint Paul that's y'all," he said bluntly. "We all got our stake in this, but We're running this together."

The room was quiet for a moment, everyone's eyes on the papers. Shoota, always the skeptic, looked at Ready. "So you're telling me we move shit up and down from Chicago, but we ain't got the same cut as Jace?" he asked, raising an eyebrow.

Ready shot him a look, his jaw set. "Nah, he's right," Saint Paul is out and Chicago is there, he said. "We ain't all gonna be equal. They got their people, we got ours. But we all gonna get a slice of the pie. Ain't no one gonna be left out."

Jace cut in. "It's about trust. The numbers ain't gonna matter if we don't trust each other, right?"

Rome, still looking at the figures, finally spoke up. "So we all gonna handle business in our own cities, but make sure the shit don't Fuck up . We ain't stepping on each other's toes."

"That's the plan," Jace said. "You get Saint Paul. We got Chicago, we took over Minneapolis and we split university , and we move like that. We move product , and cash. Everybody eats. Simple."

Enoch nodded, his voice calm but calculated. "That works. But what happens if something goes wrong? What if one of us gets hit or someone tries to flip?"

"That's where loyalty comes in," Jace said, his voice hardening. "We handle our shit. Ain't no room for weak links. And trust me, if something goes down, we handle it."

The tension in the room was thick, but the business talk was moving forward. Hit looked over at Ready, his mind working through the numbers and the plan. They were talking a good game, but he knew better than to trust everything on paper.

"Alright," Ready said finally, breaking the silence. "We are good with the numbers. But I need to know why you're really here, Jace. Why did you come to us? What's your endgame?"

Jace leaned back in his chair, hands clasped behind his head. "Simple. I'm building something bigger. I'm not just here for some quick money. I've got ties in Chicago, and I'm trying to expand. You and your crew, you got connections out here, you got the muscle and the territory. So why not join forces?"

The room absorbed the words, but Rome looked skeptical. "Alright, but we ain't trying to be no side crew to you. What's the deal with the cuts?"

Jace was ready for this. "You'll keep all the money for Saint Paul because that's y'all. We're not here to take over your blocc, we're here to work together and move products. We ain't stepping on toes, just handling business. But when it comes to Minneapolis, we split that 50/50 and university we do 70% for y'all and we take 30%. We take the city, both of us."

Shoota spoke up again and that sounded good to me. What happens when we start moving across state lines?"

Jace nodded. "That's the long-term plan. As the money flows in, we'll handle the out-of-state moves.

Y'all control Saint Paul, we'll keep Minneapolis on lock, and when it's time to expand, we push into bigger cities. But it all starts here, with the foundation we build in both cities."

As the conversation continued inside, Rome stepped out for a minute. His phone buzzed in his pocket. It was Honey, and he was already feeling the tension rising. He had enough of her games, but still, he picked up.

"What the fuck you want, Honey?" he said, his tone flat.

On the other end, Honey's voice was sweet, but there was an edge to it. "I just wanted to check in. Where are you at?"

"I'm at the warehouse, handling business," Rome snapped, pacing back and forth. "What the fuck you want?"

She paused, her voice dripping with sarcasm. "I heard y'all making moves, thought I'd see if you missed me."

Rome gritted his teeth, an annoyance building. "Don't be calling me with that bullshit, Honey. I got shit to do."

"Well, you must be out there with another bitch, huh?" Honey shot back, her tone suddenly cold.

"Don't play with me, hoe," Rome growled. "Don't ever call my phone again. Control your damn self."

He hung up without waiting for her reply, his blood boiling. He didn't know if she was working both sides or if she was just trying to cause problems, but he had enough of her games.

Back in the Warehouse

Inside, the group was still focused on the blueprint, discussing their next steps. Hit had just finished outlining the route they'd be taking, making sure everyone knew their part. But the tension in the air wasn't just from the business. Everyone knew something wasn't right.

The door creaked open, and Rome stepped back inside, his expression tight. He didn't say anything at

first, but everyone could feel the change in his demeanor.

"What's up?" Ready asked, noticing the shift in his brother.

Rome just shook his head, not in the mood to talk about Honey. "Let's finish this up. We got business to handle."

Jace raised an eyebrow, sensing the shift in energy. "Everything good?"

Rome didn't answer, his eyes flicking toward the papers again. "Yeah, everything is good. Just don't fuck with me, and we good."

The conversation continued, but the air was still thick with tension. Jace watched the crew, weighing the situation carefully. He wasn't just here for the partnership, and he had his own reasons for coming to Saint Paul. There was something more personal behind his visit.

"I'll tell you something," Jace finally spoke, breaking the silence. "I've been watching y'all for a month. Watching how y'all move. I like what I see.

Y'all make money. Y'all handle shit. But I also came here because of someone—someone who asked me to check y'all out."

Everyone exchanged glances, unsure of where this was going.

Rome squinted. "Who asked you to check us out?"

Jace leaned in. "My girl, Mocha. Y'all know her?"

It froze. Ready's eyes narrowed. They didn't expect that. "Mocha?" Ready repeated, his voice low. "That's our sister?"

Jace smiled. "Yeah. She's been filling me in on y'all. Didn't realize she was your sister though. Small world, huh?"

The room went silent for a moment as everyone processed the revelation. Jace's voice softened, more serious now. "And don't worry about her. She's my girl, and I'll make sure she's good. Ain't nobody getting close to her, not on my watch. Since I'm with her, that makes us family. I got her back, and I got yours too. We are all in this together."

Ready and Hit exchanged a look, understanding the weight of Jace's words. They both knew the risks of mixing business and family, but it wasn't just about business now. It was about loyalty.

"We appreciate that," Ready said quietly, nodding. "Mocha's family, and that means something. You show her respect, we'll do the same."

Jace's eyes hardened again. "You got it. Ain't nobody gonna mess with her. Not while I'm around."

Chapter 9

The warehouse was filled with stacks of cash and the heavy scent of smoke as HitWorld counted up the night's earnings. Hit, Ready, Rome, Enoch, Shoota, Bone, and Wild Boy were all there, going over their latest moves. Since Jace and his crew had proposed an alliance, things had only gotten more intense. They were already getting ready to expand, to make a name on both ends, but tonight there was something else pressing on their minds.

Rome's phone lit up, Honey's name flashing on the screen. He ignored it, focusing on the cash in front of him. But she called again, and again. Honey didn't know when to quit.

"Man, handle that," Hit said, nodding to the phone. "She doesn't know when to stop. Ain't nobody got time for her bullshit."

Rome let out an irritated sigh, finally picking up. "Yo, what, Honey? You blew up my line enough tonight."

"Rome, baby, don't hang up," Honey's voice was thick with desperation. "Just listen, please. I need you to talk to Hit for me. Everything got all twisted up, but you know me. You know I wouldn't cross y'all like that."

Rome scoffed. "Naw? Honey, I thought I knew you, but mfs out here saying you running around with Manny, bitch that shit that nigga did a few weeks back lookin' dead at you hoe and you tired to act like you ain't see shit You think we're stupid?"

"Rome, it ain't like that!" she pleaded, her voice shaky. "Look, I messed up, alright? I got caught up in some dumb stuff, but I never meant for it to be like this."

Rome's face twisted in anger. "Bitch, you don't know shit about loyalty. You think shit sweet bitch? Don't call my phone no more Honey. Ain't no comin' back."

Honey's tone turned desperate. "Please, Rome, you know what we had. Just give me another chance.

Rome let out a bitter laugh, glancing at the rest of the crew, who were watching with amusement. Shoota grinned, shaking his head, and Bone let out a low chuckle.

"Good for it? Honey, you are barely good for yourself. Loyalty ain't in your vocabulary," Rome spat,"HitWorld don't move like and I'm damn sure not fuckin' no bitch who ain't keep shit a bill."

"I messed up," Honey whispered, her voice shaking now. "But Rome, you know me. You know how it is out here."

Rome's jaw clenched. "Yeah, I know. I know you got yourself mixed up with them rats on University.

But don't call me again. You crossed a line, Honey, and we ain't got nothing left to talk about."

He ended the call and tossed the phone aside, irritation flashing in his eyes. Ready smirked, crossing his arms. "She really thought she could just worm her way back in, huh?"

Shoota laughed. "Some people just don't get it. She ain't loyal to nobody but herself."

Bone shook his head, arms crossed. "That's why she and the hoe's she runs with will never be one of us."

Just then, Hit's phone buzzed with a call from Lyric, who gave him the heads-up that Honey had been out there stirring up trouble, talking to anybody who'd listen, spreading HitWorld's business like it was hers to tell.

"Is she really out here thinking she can play both sides and it won't get back to us?" Hit's voice was tight, a hard edge to it. "She's about to find out real quick how we handle that."

Rome shook his head, his anger simmering. "She wanna play, we gon' show her. What the fuck it is."

Wild Boy nodded, grinning. "Ain't no room for snakes out here. She wants to play with fire, let her feel the heat."

Shoota leaned back, a dangerous gleam in his eyes. "Next time she calls, let her know she on borrowed time."

Bone smirked, his eyes cold. "This blocc's is ours. Anybody thinking otherwise can step up and find out."

"Hit leaned over and told ready to call mocha and red to put an eye on them bitches and keep them posted.

Yeah," Ready said. "Make it clear that playing games with Hit World comes with a price. I don't want her thinking she can run her mouth without consequences."

An hour later, Mocha and Red arrived, dressed in all black, their presence commanding respect without a single word spoken. He knew these two could handle business, but he didn't want to get them. Still, there was no way he was letting this slide.

Find her. Hit said even if you don't find her, find them other bitches juicy and Kiki sends a message to them hoes. Rome doesn't want to do it this way. He is in love with the bitch but y'all take care of it.

Before they was about to leave out Ready called to them "aye mocha don't think we forget cause we ain't said shit

But we will be talkin' to you about Jace.

Mocha rolled her eyes as she and Red left the warehouse.

WildBoy starts rollin up a backwood and lookin at Rome.

What the fuck is you lookin at nigga Rome said getting up already mad about how all that shit played out

I'm lookin at you sittin here lookin like you lost your best friend or somethin shorty ass a rat she been one your ass just ain't want to see that shit nigga.

Rome stood up and without hesitation he took off on WildBoy.

Hit standing there lookin'

WildBoy get Busy Bone called out.

Ready got in the middle of it and stop them what the fuck is y'all doing we brothers why the fuck y'all lettin a bitch come in between that.

Shoota and Enoch passed the blunt back and forth laughin the whole time.

"Aye Yo my bad WildBoy we brother I'm just fuck'd up in the head we coo."

Wild boy looked at Rome yea nigga we coo we brother's stop actin like Bitch.

Everyone's one of them start laughin.

Alright let's lock up and hit these streets.

Chapter 10

The vibe at Bar was still high with celebration. HitWorld and Jace's crew were toasting, laughter and chatter filling the air as they talked about the future and the money they were about to make. Drinks were flowing, the music was loud, and everyone was feeling good, but trouble always has a way of sneaking in when things seem perfect.

Rome was sitting at the bar, talking to a random woman. He barely even noticed Honey walk in with

Juicy and Kiki behind her. But Honey, already on edge, wasn't here to be ignored.

"Rome!" she shouted, her voice cutting through the music and the buzz of the bar. "What the fuck is going on with you? You actin' like you don't know me no more?"

Rome didn't even look up. He took another sip of his drink, barely acknowledging her presence. "What's up, Honey?" he muttered, his voice calm, unaffected by the tension radiating off her.

"You too busy playin' house with these hoes while you out here forgetting who held you down in the first place!" Honey sneered, stepping closer to him, putting her hand on the bar. "You act like I'm invisible now, huh?"

Mocha and Red were at a table with their brothers and the crew, talking business. But when they heard the commotion, they exchanged a quick look. Neither of them had time for this petty shit, especially not in their sister's bar. They could see it was about to go down, and they didn't want any part of Honey's drama.

But Mocha wasn't having it. As Honey's voice started to rise, Mocha stood up, her chair scraping back against the floor. Red followed her lead, her eyes locked on Honey. They had enough of Honey's mouth, and they weren't going to stand around while she disrespected Rome.

"Hold up, what the fuck did you just say?" Mocha's voice was cold, and her stance was strong, like a storm about to break. She walked up on Honey, getting in her face.

Honey's lips curled into a sneer. "I'm sayin' your bitch ass brother has been acting funny, and I'm done with it. Ain't nobody gonna keep disrespecting me."

"Bitch, shut the fuck up before you get checked," Mocha snapped, stepping closer to her. "You talkin' all that shit like you a boss, but you ain't about to disrespect my brother like that."

Red was already moving behind Honey and Kiki, juicy standing there lookin lost.

Red eyes burning with anger. "You think you're tough? Let's step outside, and we can settle this for real," Red said.

At this point, Rome finally stood up, looking over at Mocha and Red with a calm but frustrated expression. He wasn't here for the drama. "Yo, y'all need to chill. This ain't the time or the place for this shit," he said, trying to defuse the situation.

But Honey wasn't backing down. "Nah, fuck that. You think you're too good for me now, huh? You too busy with that random bitch over there to even listen to me? You really gonna let your sister and her sidekick talk to me like this?" Her voice was louder now, cutting through the tension.

Just as the situation was about to escalate, Jace stepped into the middle of it all. He had been watching the entire scene unfold, his eyes moving between Mocha, Red, and Honey. He didn't want to see anyone getting hurt, especially not in a place where business had just been laid out and deals were being made.

"Alright, alright, hold up!" Jace's deep voice cut through the noise as he stepped in between them. "This shit is done, y'all hoe's find somethin safe to Do mocha baby Let's go chill."

He grabbed Juicy by the arm and pulled her away from the commotion. "You bitches better leave before I lay one of you punk-ass hoes down for

Good," Jace warned them, his tone sharp. He didn't give a damn who they were or where they came from—disrespect was never going to be tolerated. He wasn't about to let some petty drama get in the way of the bigger picture.

Kiki, looking nervous, stepped back. She didn't want any part of this heat juicy either. Honey, however, wasn't done.

"You don't control shit, Jace. Don't you ever put your hands on me or my girls again," Honey snarled, but Jace wasn't fazed.

"I don't give a fuck who you are," he snapped back. "But you better learn some damn respect. If you think you're gonna keep running your mouth like that, you'll get handled just like the rest."

Red and Mocha were still standing there, not backing down, but watching the interaction carefully. They knew this wasn't the time to add fuel to the fire, especially when Jace was involved.

With the tension still hanging in the air, Jace took a step back, his eyes moving to Mocha and Red. "This shit ain't over, but it's damn sure over for tonight," Jace said, looking at Mocha. "Will we handle this another time?"

Mocha, still fuming but with a sense of control, nodded toward Jace. "We'll leave it," she said, her voice steady. "But don't let it happen again."

With that, the scene began to settle, the crowd breaking up as people tried to return to the night. But the message had been made loud and clear: disrespect HitWorld, and there would be consequences. And as for Honey, Kiki, and Juicy—they'd just learned a hard lesson.

As Honey, Juicy, and Kiki walked out of the bar, Honey pulled out her phone. Her anger was still burning, and she wasn't done with Rome just yet. She hit the dial and waited for him to pick up.

Rome's phone rang twice before he answered, his voice cold. "What now, Honey?"

"You know what's up, Rome," Honey said through gritted teeth. "I'm out here, and I want answers. You think you can just forget about me?"

Rome didn't waste time with words. "I ain't got time for this shit tonight. You already know what it is. Don't call me again."

With that, Rome ended the call without a second thought.

Honey seethed, looking down at the phone in her hand. This wasn't over. Not by a long shot.

Meanwhile, Hit and Ready were standing near the bar, watching the situation unfold. They exchanged a look, then turned to Jace.

"I like how you stepped in for our sisters' respect," Hit said, nodding. "That shows you have a heart. We can work together and get this money."

Ready added, "For real. That's real loyalty, and we don't take that lightly. Let's keep it moving and get this cash, no more distractions."

Jace smiled, his crew behind him. "I respect that. We are good. Let's make some moves."

Chapter 11

The frustration from last night still lingered in the air. Mocha couldn't let it go. The disrespect from Honey and her crew was one thing, but the fact that Rome had just sat back and did nothing about it? That was something else entirely. The more she thought about it, the angrier she got. Mocha couldn't afford to keep waiting for Rome to handle his business. She was done.

Mocha sat in her high-rise apartment, scrolling through her phone when she saw the messages from her brothers—Hit and Ready. They'd been texting nonstop since last night. Ready had a habit of checking in on her. The love they shared was unspoken, but it ran deep.

The doorbell rang, pulling Mocha out of her thoughts. She walked over and opened the door to find her brothers standing there. Hit gave her a nod, his eyes sharp, while Ready stepped inside, his expression serious.

"Good morning, sis," Ready said, his tone steady. "What's the play?"

"Last night was bullshit," Mocha said, walking over to the couch. She threw herself down, her frustration bubbling up again. "Honey and her crew came in here acting like they run shit. I tried to stay calm, but I'm done. It's time to handle it."

Hit and Ready exchanged a look, the kind of silent communication that only siblings would understand. Then Hit spoke, his voice calm but sharp as a blade.

"Rome ain't doing shit about it, huh?"

"Nope." Mocha's voice was tight. "And if he's not gonna handle it, I will."

Ready nodded slowly. "You know I got your back. We can handle that bitch. But Rome's gotta step up. He can't just let his girl talk crazy and not do anything about it."

Mocha let out a frustrated breath. "I know. But I can't wait on him forever. I've been doing that, and it's gotten us nowhere. He's too damn blind to see what's really going on."

Hit nodded again. "We handle things the right way. But if Rome ain't gonna make a move, we'll make sure it gets done. Family comes first. Always."

"I'll make sure she knows what happens when you cross us," Ready added, his voice colder than usual.

Mocha glanced up at her brothers, relieved that they understood. She wasn't alone in this. "I'm glad y'all got my back. But I need to know—do we take care of Rome too, or just Honey?"

Ready shook his head. "We don't handle Rome. He's family. But if he can't step up, that's on him. You already know what's gonna happen if he lets this shit slide again."

Hit stayed quiet for a moment before finally speaking. "We deal with Honey first. Once that's handled, we let Rome know what's up. He'll have to decide where his loyalty lies."

Mocha's eyes hardened as she thought about the situation. "We'll put her in her place, but Rome needs to understand that I'm not playing anymore. He can't keep letting her disrespect me like this."

The tension in the room was thick when the doorbell rang again. This time, Mocha didn't even need to look to know who it was. She could hear the familiar sound of Rome's footsteps in the hallway before the door creaked open.

"Yo," Rome's voice echoed as he stepped inside, his eyes scanning the room.

Mocha stood up, her anger boiling over. "You're the last person I wanna talk to right now," she shot back. "What the hell happened last night, Rome? That shit made us look weak in front of Jace and his crew."

Rome winced at her words. "Look, I was just trying to avoid any drama. You know how Honey is."

Mocha shook her head, the anger rising in her chest. "You didn't avoid shit. You let that bitch walk all over me. That ain't how we do things. I don't care if she's your girl. You can't let her disrespect me like that, especially not in front of Jace."

Ready spoke up, his voice low but deadly. "You should've stepped up, Rome. You didn't. And now we gotta clean up the mess."

Rome's eyes flicked between Mocha and Ready, then he looked down at the floor, a hint of regret crossing his features. "I know. I fucked up. I should've said something."

Hit, who had been quiet until now, crossed his arms. "That ain't enough. You gotta step up, bro. This is family. If you're gonna be with her, that's on you, but don't let her drag us down with her."

Mocha's gaze locked onto Rome's, her expression cold. "If you don't handle her, I will. I'm done being patient. I'm done waiting for you."

Rome's jaw tightened. "I'll handle it. Just don't go overboard, Mocha. I got this."

Mocha didn't respond right away. She just stared at him, weighing his words. Then she nodded once, but her expression didn't soften. "You better. Because if I have to step in again, there won't be any more talking. It's straight up business."

Rome exhaled, his shoulders slumping as if the weight of the conversation had hit him. "I hear you."

"Good." Mocha's voice was firm, resolute. "Because I'm not about to let that bitch keep disrespecting me. She doesn't get to cross me and get away with it."

Ready and Hit exchanged another glance, and then Ready stepped forward. "Let's make this right. We don't let shit slide in this family."

Mocha gave a short nod. "Yeah, we don't. And I'm not gonna let it happen again. Let's handle this, and we'll deal with the rest later."

Rome gave her a brief nod before turning to leave. "I'll take care of it. I promise."

As the door clicked shut behind him, Mocha let out a long breath, her anger still simmering but knowing the next steps had to be taken carefully. It wasn't just about Honey anymore—it was about making sure Rome knew his place in this family, and that when shit went down, he needed to be a part of handling it.

Ready and Hit both stood, their expressions hard, and Mocha knew they were ready to back her up—no matter what came next.

Chapter 12

The whole crew arrived at 3rd Street Bar, where Lyric was waiting at a corner table. The vibe in the place was thick with anticipation, HitWorld filling out the space as they settled in. Lyric looked serious, nodding to Hit as he slid into the booth next to her.

"Look," Lyric began, her voice low, "I got word Manny and Minneapolis, about to run up on one of the spot's.

But that ain't all." She leaned in closer. Mocha called and said "Jace and his boys are pulling up any minute. He wants to meet, drop off the goods, and see how this goes with everyone in one place."

As if on cue, the door opened, and Jace walked in with his crew, carrying a presence that turned heads. Hit and Ready exchanged a look, then stood up to meet him.

"What's good, fam?" Hit greeted, extending a hand. Jace took it, and they exchanged a solid dap.

Behind him, a couple of his boys were carrying duffle bags, heavy with something valuable.

"Had to bring y'all a little gift," Jace said, motioning for his crew to set the bags on the table. He unzipped one of them, revealing bundles of cash stacked alongside neatly bagged packages of powder. Next to it were keys, each with a different emblem, marking cars parked nearby.

"We're makin' moves, and I need people I trust to handle the flow," Jace said, looking at each member. "This is for y'all, Keys to different cars to keep everything in rotation. Different rides for different days. No one's gonna clock your moves."

Hit scanned the duffle bags, then nodded. "You came through, Jace. Ain't no doubts on our end about this."

Jace's expression shifted, growing more serious. "Good. But I need to talk to you one-on-one, Hit. Away from all the eyes. Mocha's apartment—neutral ground, yeah?"

Hit's brow furrowed, but he nodded slowly. "Alright. I'll hear you out there."

The whole crew arrived at 3rd Street Bar, where Lyric was waiting at a corner table. The vibe in the place was thick with anticipation, HitWorld filling out the space as they settled in. Lyric looked serious, nodding to Hit as he slid into the booth next to her.

"Look," Lyric began, her voice low, "I got word Thomas Hittas been running moves up on University, close to your blocc. They're not just holding down spots; they're making new alliances with Minneapolis. But that ain't all." She leaned in closer. "Jace and his boys are pulling up any minute. He wants to meet, drop off the goods, and see this through with everyone in one place."

As if on cue, the door opened, and Jace walked in with his crew, carrying a presence that turned heads. Hit and Ready exchanged a look, then stood up to meet him.

"What's good, fam?" Hit greeted, extending a hand. Jace took it, and they exchanged a solid dap. Behind him, a couple of his boys were carrying duffle bags, heavy with something valuable.

"Had to bring y'all a little gift," Jace said, motioning for his crew to set the bags on the table. He unzipped one of them, revealing bundles of cash stacked alongside neatly bagged packages of powder. Next to it were keys, each with a different emblem, marking cars parked nearby.

"We're makin' moves, and I need people I trust to handle the flow," Jace said, looking at each member of HitWorld. "This is for you, your people, and every spot we lock down together. Keys to different cars to keep everything in rotation. Different rides for different days. No one's gonna clock your moves."

Hit scanned the duffle bags, then nodded. "You came through, Jace. Ain't no doubts on our end about this."

Jace's expression shifted, growing more serious. "Good. But I need to talk to you one-on-one, Hit. Away from all the eyes. Mocha's apartment—neutral ground, yeah?"

Hit's brow furrowed, but he nodded slowly. "Alright. I'll hear you out there."

Ready, picking up on the vibe, asked, "What's this about, though? If it's serious, we will all be in it together."

Jace raised a hand. "Respect, but this ain't nothin' against the rest of y'all. Just need a moment with your boy here. Don't worry—I'm still here for business."

Ready exchanged a glance with Hit, then nodded. "If Hit's good with it, we all good."

Jace looked at his crew. "Aight, fellas, let's get situated with what we brought. Y'all meet back at the spot. I'll catch up with Hit once I've said my piece."

With that, Jace's guys filed out, leaving the crew alone with the duffles. Bone was the first to speak up after they left. "So, we trustin' this, right?"

Hit shot him a look. "This is about building something bigger. Jace got the plug to take us from what we doin' to something that runs deep. If we don't take this, someone else will. But if he's playin' with us, we'll find out soon enough."

Rome nodded, eyeing the bags. "We move smart, split the routes, and play it just like he laid it out. Every key has its own route, its own people."

"Exactly," Hit agreed. "The cars switch out every week. Ain't nobody can trace us if we keep it movin'."

Lyric watched them with approval. "Y'all got this handled. But don't lose sight of Manny's crew. They're just waitin' for a slip."

Bone nodded, gripping one of the keys. "Let's handle the blocc first and secure what's ours. Then we take it to the next level with Jace."

An hour later, Hit met Jace at Mocha's apartment. Jace was already waiting inside, a drink in hand, looking out the window. When he turned, his gaze was all business.

"Good you came," Jace said, setting the glass down. "I didn't want to say this in front of your whole crew 'cause I need you to understand how serious this is."

Hit crossed his arms. "Speak your mind."

Jace took a breath. "I came here to make money, expand, all that. But there's something else, too. I'm with your sister, Mocha."

Hit's face hardened, but he didn't interrupt. He just held Jace's gaze, waiting.

"Look, I know how this looks," Jace continued, "but I didn't come into the picture with no games. Mocha's my girl, and I'm here because she wanted me to be here. She's loyal, man. She wanted me to see how you run things. She said y'all were family, and I respect that. I had to come see for myself before making any moves with you."

Hit finally spoke, his voice steady but cold. "So you're here, sayin' you're with Mocha. And now what?"

Jace took a step closer, his voice lowering. "Now? Now I'm tellin' you nobody will touch her. Ain't nobody gonna get close to her. I got her, just like I got your back if we were in this together. You got my word."

Hit took a moment, then gave a short nod. "Aight. We family now, then. If you're serious about this, you're serious about us. But if you ever cross her, or cross us, that's it."

Jace met his eyes, no hesitation. "Understood. But know this, Hit—I'm here to build somethin' solid. We take care of Mocha, and we take care of business. We're on the same page."

They stood in silence for a beat, a mutual understanding passing between them.

"Now let's get this money," Hit finally said, his expression softening slightly.

Jace extended his hand, and they shook, sealing the deal as both allies and family. Whatever came next, they'd face it together, ready to run Saint Paul and Chicago as a united force.

you're serious about us. But if you ever cross her, or cross us, that's it."

Jace met his eyes, no hesitation. "Understood. But know this, Hit—I'm here to build somethin' solid. We take care of Mocha, and we take care of business. We're on the same page."

They stood in silence for a beat, a mutual understanding passing between them.

"Now let's get this money," Hit finally said, his expression softening slightly.

Jace extended his hand, and they shook, sealing the deal as both allies and family. Whatever came next, they'd face it together, ready to run Saint Paul and Chicago as a united force.

Chapter 13

The next night, HitWorld gathered at the warehouse for their latest meeting with Jace and his crew. The dim lights cast long shadows across the room, adding to the tension and anticipation in the air. This wasn't just a regular meetup; tonight, they were talking power moves, the kind of decisions that could shift control of the streets.

Hit leaned against a crate, watching as Jace and his crew rolled in. Ready, Rome, Bone, Wild Boy,

Shoota, and Enoch were already scattered around the warehouse, keeping their eyes sharp and their voices low. When Jace stepped in, he dropped a thick folder on the table, filled with routes, stash locations, and contact info. It was everything they needed to solidify the partnership.

"Here's the setup," Jace started, taking a seat across from Hit. "Routes from Saint Paul to Chicago, checkpoints, contacts, and safe houses. We're covering ground that nobody else can touch."

Hit nodded, flipping through the folder. "Solid work, Jace. You ain't playin'."

"Nah, I don't play when it comes to this," Jace replied, his tone serious. "We got eyes on every move and the right people on the payroll. Ain't nobody slippin'."

Rome glanced up from his seat, skeptical. "Sounds good, but are you sure your boys can handle business on our side? Saint Paul ain't no joke."

Jace returned the look, unfazed. "I wouldn't be here if I wasn't sure. You keep your end tight, we'll handle ours."

Ready leaned forward, breaking down the logistics. "So how's the split lookin'?"

Jace pointed to the folder. We already talked about it. We keep on' it the same "Saint Paul's yours, Chicago's is ours, we take 30%. From university, we split Minneapolis 50-50."

Bone smirked, drumming his fingers on the table. "So speakin' of University? We takin' it over, or we lettin' Manny and his crew keep it and make them work for us?"

Jace looked at him dead-on. "We pushin' in, but smart. No need to set off alarms yet. We keep things quiet, let 'em get comfortable, then we sweep."

Rome cracked a grin. "Sounds like a plan. We been wantin' that blocc for a minute."

Just then, Lyrics call interrupted the meeting. Hit stepped away to take it, coming back with a serious look. "Lyric says that Manny is lurkin' around the blocc tonight, makin' noise."

Enoch shrugged. "Let 'em. They ain't ready for what's comin'."

Jace nodded, his face set. "Let's finish up here, and then we handle them. We all in?"

One by one, the men nodded. Hit reached across the table, with a firm handshake to Jace.

Everyone went to different blocc's Hit and Ready hopped into the Chevy pullin' up to Westminster where Scrappy, the lookout who had been watching the corners, stepped up to the car window. "I caught some chatter on the street.

"Aye yea what's that Rwadt said.

Word is, Manny and his crew about to make some noise soon and to pass the message to HitWorld lettin y'all know that y'all time is up

Hit start laughin." Ready looked over with a grin on his face.

Ready called WildBoy

WildBoy ain't answering Ready sent him a message " Keep y'all eyes open out there.

As the night wore on, Hit remained restless.

As the crew rallied together, Hit felt the tension ease slightly. They were all in this together, and he knew they'd protect what they had built.

As they stood there, Ready leaned closer to Hit. "We need to get ahead of Manny before it spirals out of control. If Minneapolis gettin' involved, it's gonna get ugly." For sure.

Chapter 14

The next day, HitWorld was all business. The crew hit the ground early, moving from their usual spots, stacking that money as they handled the new load Jace had dropped on them. It was a different kind of weight, heavy and serious, and they knew this partnership with Jace wasn't just for show. Today was about pushing the work hard and making that cash flow, all while watching each other's backs.

Hit was driving with Ready in the passenger seat, both of them silent as they planned out the day's moves. The city streets were already busy, but they had their route mapped out, each stop precise and efficient. Just as they rolled up to a red light, Hit's phone buzzed, breaking the silence. Jace's name flashed across the screen, and Hit swiped to answer.

"Yo," Hit said, his voice steady. He already knew if Jace was calling this early, he had something lined up.

"Hit, we 'bout to head out to Minneapolis, check out the blocc," Jace said on the other end. "I got my crew, and we're about to put some eyes on Manny and his crew. His people think they run it, but we gotta see how tight they really hold it down."

Jace let out a short laugh. "You know me, Hit. I'm out here scoping for now. If they step out of line, though, it's gonna be handled."

"Bet," Hit replied, a hint of respect in his tone. "You find anything worth actin' on, hit me up. We got the Eastside on lock today, so if Minneapolis lookin' good, we'll roll through when the time's right."

"Say less," Jace said, the call ending with an unspoken understanding. Both crews knew the stakes, and neither was playing games.

Hit put his phone down, and Ready shot him a look. "They tryna see what Manny and Minneapolis are up to? They gon' take that as a threat. Jace better be ready to make it known that he's not messin' around."

"Exactly," Hit agreed, eyes fixed on the road. "It's a test, but if they push, Jace and his boys ain't gonna back down. They're gonna make that clear, one way or another."

The car fell back into silence as they continued their route. They made stops at a couple of their usual spots, checking in on the product, counting stacks, and ensuring everything was running smoothly. They knew that today was critical with lurking in the background, waiting for any slip-up to make a move. But HitWorld wasn't about to give them that satisfaction.

Around noon, they met up with the rest of the crew at a spot over on the Eastside. Wild Boy, Shoota, Bone, and Enoch were all there, each of them keeping an eye on the street, waiting for the next move.

"Jace just hit me up," Hit told them as he stepped out of his car, lighting a cigarette. "Him and his boys are checkin' Manny and his crew

Out today. They wanna see what 's going on ."

Shoota laughed, crossing his arms. "Man, that's gon' be fireworks if they catch wind of Jace's crew. You know they've been layin' low, but that's their spot."

Wild Boy shrugged. "They gon' either show respect or get checked. Simple as that."

Bone nodded, glancing at Hit. "And if they get bold?"

"Then it's on," Hit replied, his tone calm but firm. "But Jace knows what he's doing. He ain't new to this."

Just then, Hit phone buzzed, and he glanced at the screen. "It's Lyric. She wants us to stop by the bar later. Said some niggas been around, asking questions."

Ready raised an eyebrow. "Questions? 'Bout what?"

Hit shrugged, slipping his phone back in his pocket. "Didn't say, but she sounded on edge. Tell her we'll pull through later, make sure it's nothing."

Hit looked around at the crew, his expression serious. "Alright, we finish up here, then we slide by the bar. Make sure nobody tryna mess with Lyric's spot. This whole thing with Thomas Hitta got people actin' bold."

They split up again, each of them moving with a purpose as they checked off the rest of their tasks for the day. As they wrapped things up, they all piled into their cars and headed to Lyric's bar on 3rd Street. By the time they arrived, the evening crowd was just starting to trickle in.

Inside, the bar had that usual dim vibe, with Lyric behind the counter, giving a nod to Hit as he walked in. "Glad y'all here," she said, her eyes scanning the room.

"What's goin' on?" Hit asked, sliding onto a barstool while the others spread out, keeping a close watch on the place.

"Some dudes came by earlier. Said they were 'lookin' for somebody who runs things.' Ain't never seen 'em around before, but they were definitely tryna size me up," Lyric explained.

Hit clenched his jaw. "They mention any names?"

Lyric shook her head. "Nah, but they was hintin' around, asking who handles the Eastside."

Ready shook his head, his expression darkening. "Sounds like somebody tryna send a message."

"Well, we got one too," Hit said, his voice low but firm. "Ain't nobody gon' step in here and press you for information, not while HitWorld is around. They come back, you let us know."

Lyric nodded, a hint of relief in her eyes. "Y'all always got my back."

"Always," Hit replied. He glanced at the rest of the crew, a silent agreement passing between them.

They stayed at the bar for a while, keeping an eye on things until the evening crowd picked up and it was clear there'd be no more trouble for the night. By the time they left, the crew was feeling more on edge than usual, aware that this was only the beginning.

Back in the car, Hit checked his phone, half expecting a message from Jace or another tip-off about Manny's crew. But for now, all was quiet. Still, he knew it wouldn't stay that way for long.

"Tomorrow's another day," he said to Ready as they drove off into the night. "But one thing's clear—they watchin'. We just gotta stay one step ahead."

Chapter 15

The crew was posted up at Sunray, as usual. Hit, Ready, Wild Boy, Rome, Bone, Shoota, and Enoch stood in the middle of the blocc, eyes scanning the area, watching the flow of traffic and making sure no one was stepping out of linc. The hustle never stopped, and neither did the grind. But today was different. Jace had called Hit earlier, letting him know he was coming through with some more product, and he'd be bringing a few familiar faces with him.

Hit didn't hesitate. He gathered the crew and made sure everything was tight. They knew what time it was. ain't no time for fuck ups , and they had business to handle.

The low rumble of Jace's black SUV pulled into the lot, and the crew immediately knew it was him. As the SUV came to a stop, the crew's eyes locked on the familiar faces in the backseat: Mocha and Red, Hit and Ready's sisters. They were in the car with Jace. That was all it took to set the tone.

Jace stepped out first, popping the trunk to reveal bags of product neatly stacked in the back. The scent of high-quality work hit the air instantly. He tossed a few bags to Bone and Shoota, and they caught them without a second thought.

"Got the goods," Jace said with a grin. "More work, more heat. You know how we do."

Rome stepped up, his eyes narrowing. "We ain't worried about them. But if they wanna test us, we'll show them what it is."

Jace shot him a grin. "I like that. I brought Mocha and Red, they've been talking to me. And I trust Mocha . We're family now, for real."

Mocha and Red didn't say much. They stood beside Jace, both of them looking tough, but there was no mistaking the pride they felt as they watched their brothers work. The bond between family and business was tight, and they knew what was at stake.

Hit nodded, "Appreciate that, Jace. But we ain't just about moving weight. We need to make sure we're handling business on all fronts. Minneapolis can't think they can just come in and take over either."

"Exactly," Jace said, locking eyes with Hit. "I'm just making sure your people are straight. I don't want any misunderstandings. It won't be trust me."

As they discussed the next steps, Jace's phone buzzed, pulling his attention for a moment. He glanced at it quickly and looked back at the crew. "One of my people's out there. I'll check in with them later, but for now, let's talk shop."

Mocha and Red exchanged looks before Mocha stepped forward. "So what's the move, Jace? What's the plan?"

Jace smiled, clearly liking the question. "Simple. We move in. The crew out there is too slow, too messy. We clean up, take the game over, and make sure nobody can step to us. We're gonna build something bigger than just these cities—we make it all ours."

Ready's eyes hardened as he nodded. "Sounds like a plan. But we'll need to make sure we got everything understood."

Jace's grin widened.

The whole crew was quiet for a moment, taking it all in. They all knew that the game was about more than just the streets. It was about power. Money. And making sure that their name stayed at the top of the food chain.

Jace walked over to Mocha and Red, giving them a look that spoke volumes. "Your brothers are ready. Now we just need to make sure we keep everything tight. No mistakes."

Mocha nodded, her voice low but steady. "They got this. Just make sure you handle your end."

With that, Jace turned and gave a final nod to the crew. "I'll be in touch. Let's keep moving. The city's ours if we want it."

As Jace and his crew got in the SUV and drove off, HitWorld stood in the lot, looking at the bags of product in their hands, and the future they had just locked in. The streets were about to get hotter, and with Jace by their side, they knew they were about to make moves that would change everything.

"Let's get to work," Ready said, his voice low and serious.

And with that, HitWorld moved forward, ready.

Everyone spit up the product and moved to their location's.

Rome and WildBoy were posted up on old Hudson when they spotted reek ass comin' out one of the buildings over there.

Rome oh hell yeah get that nigga.

Wild Boy He stepped into the doorway, gun raised. "Yo, Reek!"

Reek froze, his eyes going wide as he saw WildBoy and Rome blockin' the exit. His cocky grin vanished, replaced by panic.

"WildBoy—man, it's not what it looks like!" Reek stammered, hands raised in surrender.

"Oh, it's exactly what it looks like," Rome cut in, voice cold and steady. Manny has been sending messages throwing mfs where he at now Rome said naw Rome you got it all wrong reek said. It was that bitch Honey, and her little crew been comin' back tellin' Manny shit and y'all move?

    WildBoy shot Rome a dirty ass look.

    Reek's face paled, his eyes darting between WildBoy and Rome. you got it twisted. I wasn't sayin' nothin.

    Rome punched his ass in the mouth tell Manny we said we comin' for him.

Chapter 16

The night in Westminster was tense. The usual hum of the streets felt different tonight. There was an undeniable pressure in the air—like the calm before a storm. HitWorld, standing firm on their blocc, had been preparing for a shift. The partnership with Jace and his crew was solid, but something had shifted in the atmosphere. Word had been getting around that Thomas Hitta's crew was moving in with their own plans, and Minneapolis was aligning with them.

Hit, Ready, Wild Boy, Bone, Shoota, Enoch, and Rome were gathered in their usual spot, scanning the street for any signs of trouble. They knew the game was about to change, but nobody could have predicted how fast.

"Something's off, Hit," Ready said quietly. He wasn't one to jump to conclusions, but the way things were unfolding didn't feel like business as usual.

"I know," Hit replied, his eyes scanning the street. "We've been hearing rumblings from Minneapolis, but I didn't expect them to come this hard. Manny has been making moves, and now they're bringing

Minneapolis into the picture. This ain't just a street war. This is bigger than that."

As they spoke, the sound of engines roaring in the distance sent a chill through the crew. They all turned their heads in unison. The rumble was getting closer. The headlights of a few cars came into view, and Hit's instincts immediately kicked in.

The first car pulled into view—familiar black SUVs with tinted windows. The unmistakable insignia of one of Manny's crew was plastered all over the vehicles. Behind them, another set of cars followed: Minneapolis muscle, joining forces to push in on their territory.

As the cars came to a stop, doors slammed open, and men started pouring out, armed and ready for war. The crew moved into position, their eyes sharp, adrenaline coursing through their veins. Jace and his crew were on the opposite side of the street, waiting. They'd been a part of this, but now, they were caught in the middle. The enemy had arrived, and the night

The sound of gunfire echoed through Westminster, the night filled with chaos and bloodshed as HitWorld and Jace's crew fought to hold their ground. Manny's crew, along with Minneapolis, had come at them hard, trying to take control of the blocc. But HitWorld wasn't about to let anyone step on their blocc, and neither was Jace and his crew.

Jace had already proven he could hold his own, but tonight, it was clear that he wasn't just here to make deals. His crew wasn't just backing him up—they were in this to win it, and they weren't going down easy.

"Get those niggas off our blocc!" Hit shouted, a steady presence as he popped off rounds. His eyes were focused, tracking every movement, every shot fired.

Jace and his boys were right beside HitWorld, taking down some Minneapolis hooters who had pushed too close. They weren't just standing there—they were active, moving fast, clearing their side of the street, and letting off shots that found their marks. A few of the Minneapolis muscle dropped in quick succession, their bodies crumpling to the pavement.

"Fuck them niggas up!" Wild Boy yelled, his voice filled with adrenaline as he took down two more from Manny's crew. "They're gonna learn today!"

The street lit up with flashes of gunfire, and every shot taken felt like it was another step closer to victory. But just like that, Wild Boy caught a bullet in his leg. He collapsed to the ground, his face contorted in pain, but he didn't stop firing.

"Fuck! I'm good!" Wild Boy shouted, gritting his teeth. His leg wasn't slowing him down yet.

Shoota, moving with the precision of a seasoned soldier, took out another two shooters from Minneapolis, but in the process, a bullet grazed his arm. He winced but kept his eyes locked on the targets.

"Fuck this, we need to finish them off," Shoota growled, still firing back despite the wound.

Rome, who had been standing alongside HitWorld, watched the shit unfold. His eyes narrowed as another wave of Manny's crew tried to advance. But it wasn't just the enemy shooters that caught his attention.

"There's too many of them," Rome said to Hit, eyes darting around the street. "We need to get more aggressive or they're gonna overrun us."

Hit gave him a sharp nod. "They'll break. Just keep pushing." He glanced at Bone. "Don't let up!"

Enoch was keeping the perimeter secure, watching for any more shooters who might try to flank their position. His gaze was sharp, catching movement in the distance. "They're trying to regroup, we need to move fast."

"Let's go!" Hit called, leading the charge. He moved with the precision of a general, cutting down more of Manny's men. The street was thick with gunpowder and smoke, but HitWorld was slowly pushing them back.

Jace, staying close to Hit, wasn't letting up either. He was methodical, each shot taken with purpose. He wasn't here to just make noise; he was here to show them who was in control.

"Your crew's handling it, Jace," Hit said, firing at a few men trying to retreat. "But don't get cocky. We gotta finish this."

Jace's lips curled into a grin. "Ain't no backing down now." He turned, firing at another shooter from Minneapolis.

As the tide of the battle shifted, the enemies from Thomas Hitta's crew began to break. They weren't prepared for HitWorld's relentless offense, and they started falling back. But just as they thought they were winning, the sound of more engines revving filled the air.

"Shit! More backup!" Hit shouted.

But before they could regroup, the fight escalated. A loud shout rang out from across the street. "We ain't done yet!"

Hit turned to see more of Manny's shooters pushing in from the rear. The war wasn't over.

"Move!" Hit shouted. "We push them back now!"

They couldn't afford to get complacent. The fight raged on, and just as things seemed to calm, another wave of shots rang out from the other side. More enemies were coming, this time with reinforcements from Minneapolis.

Wild Boy gritted his teeth, still on the ground. "We need to end this."

Rome, looking over at Wild Boy, snarled, "We finish this or we're gonna keep getting hit."

Jace, seeing the desperation in the air, signaled his crew to keep up the pressure. He moved forward with Hit, firing off rounds at any movement he could see. They weren't about to let Manny's crew and Minneapolis take over.

"Rome, help me cover the back," Jace said, his voice steady despite the intensity of the situation.

Rome nodded and sprinted over to cover Jace, both of them laying down fire as they took out the remaining shooters from Manny's crew.

The two crews, working side by side, pressed forward with precision. Jace's crew took down three more men from Minneapolis in one clean sweep, but it wasn't over yet.

"Let's finish this!" Hit growled, charging forward, his gun steady. "Get those last few down, and we're done."

But that didn't stop there. Just when they thought the fight was dying down, a stray bullet hit Shoota in the arm, sending him to his knees with a shout of pain. He didn't go down, though—he kept firing, covering his boys as best as he could.

"Get that shit under control!" Hit barked, but he was still pushing forward, taking out another shooter from Manny's side.

"Don't worry about me," Shoota grunted, fighting through the pain. "We ain't losing this."

The gunfire started to die down as HitWorld and Jace's crew took out the last few members of Manny's crew. The streets were filled with smoke, and the ground was littered with bodies, but they had done it.

The battle for Westminster was over—for now.

Hit turned to Jace, wiping the sweat from his forehead, and gave him a sharp look. "You did good out here."

Jace, breathing heavily, nodded. "Ain't nobody messing with us now."

But the fight wasn't over. They'd secured their turf for the moment, but more would come. There was no peace when you ran a blocc—only the promise of war, and in the streets, it was either kill or be killed.

"Let's get our boys patched up," Hit said, looking over at Wild Boy and Shoota. "Then we talk about the next move."

As the adrenaline wore off, everyone stood together, looking out over the carnage. They had won this round, but it was clear: the game was far from over.

Chapter 17

The sound of tires screeching echoed through the streets as HitWorld and Jace's crew raced away from Westminster. The shootout had escalated quickly, leaving bodies in their wake and the streets hot with the smell of gunpowder and adrenaline. With the cops likely already on their way, there was no time to waste.

"Get to Mocha's," Hit said, his voice low. "We need to lay low for a minute. Figure out our next move."

Rome nodded, already pulling out his phone.

He sent a quick text to Lyric, telling her to get Kaliyah and Red to Mocha's high-rise apartment. They needed backup—medical help and Wild Boy had been hit in the leg, and Shoota wasn't looking much better, with a bullet wound to the arm.

Mocha's apartment was the safest place for them right now. It was far enough from the streets of Westminster but still close enough to make a quick getaway if things went south. Hit knew Mocha had the space, the privacy, and the right connections to handle things in the shadows.

As they neared the high-rise, Hit quickly pulled out his phone and sent a message to Mocha: *We're on the way. Jace and his crew are with us. I'll talk to you when we get there. We need to lay low.* The message was sent with a buzz, and Hit turned to the crew.

The car swerved into the underground garage of the high-rise, and the team quickly exited, careful not to draw attention to themselves. They made their way to the elevator, heads low and eyes sharp. When the doors opened, they were greeted by Mocha, who had clearly been expecting them.

Her face was calm, but there was a noticeable tension in her eyes. She stepped forward as they entered the spacious lobby of the high-rise, her voice low and focused.

"Get them inside, quick. What happened out there?" she asked, looking between the crew.

Hit spoke first. "The Minneapolis crew showed up with heat. We weren't expecting it to go down like that. Wild Boy and Shoota got hit."

Mocha's eyes flickered to Shoota and Wild Boy, who were leaning against the walls, trying to stay steady despite the pain. "Shit. We need to get you two cleaned up."

Lyric, Red, and Kaliyah entered the apartment a few moments later. Lyric wasted no time and immediately went to Wild Boy, checking his leg. Kaliyah quickly followed, and both women worked quickly to get the wounds treated. Red, however, hung back, eyes sharp and watching the room. She knew things were about to get real.

Shoota was in the corner, his arm bandaged up but still in pain. "We gotta get back out there. We ain't done yet," he muttered, his tone full of determination.

Mocha shot him a look, her eyes hard. "You both need to chill. We ain't moving until Kaliyah says you're good."

Kaliyah worked fast, stitching up Wild Boy's leg. "He's gonna be fine, but he needs rest. Shoota's gonna be alright, too, but we gotta get you both off your feet for a minute."

Hit, Ready, Bone, and Enoch and Jace crew took a seat around the room, watching their wounded brothers while keeping a close eye on the door. Jace stood by the window, his hand on his chin as he thought about what had just gone down.

"You think this is the end of it?" Bone asked, his voice low but heavy with tension. "Cause those motherfuckers didn't back down."

"Nah," Ready said, shaking his head. "They're gonna keep coming. But now they know we ain't no pussy's . We're making a statement. They hit us first, but we took some niggas down."

Hit was staring at the floor, his mind working through the next steps. "We need to get ourselves together. Can't let the cops find us here. The heat's already on its way."

Just as he finished speaking, the sound of tires screeching echoed from the street below. Hit stood up, motioning for the others to stay quiet. "That's our cue," he said, his voice calm but authoritative. "We gotta move now."

Mocha looked at him, her expression serious. "You better get out of here before the heat arrives. But be careful—if they're looking for us, they'll be coming for you, too."

"Thanks, Mocha," Hit said, his voice softening for a moment. "We'll be back. Just keep everything tight. Don't trust no one outside of HitWorld and the crew."

Jace nodded in agreement. "We got this. But I'll be honest with you—those Minneapolis niggas aren't gonna stop until we take 'em down for good."

Lyric and Red stood by the door, ready to head out. "We'll keep things locked down here. You handle your shit out there, and we'll be ready when you get back," Red said.

With that, the crew began to make their way toward the exit. Hit, Ready, Rome , Bone, and Enoch moved swiftly but quietly, careful not to attract any unwanted attention. Mocha and the others stayed behind, keeping their heads low, watching as the crew disappeared into the night.

Chapter 18

The days following the shootout left everyone on edge. Wild Boy and Shoota were still recovering, but the fire in their eyes showed they were ready to get back in action. They'd all gathered at Mocha's high-rise, her spot feeling like a safe haven, at least for now.

Hit leaned back, his expression hard as he ran through the events of that day in his mind. "We gotta move smarter, real talk," he said, looking around at his brothers. "Those fools ain't letting up, and now they got help from across the river. We're in this deep."

Ready, his sister Red, and Kaliyah were scattered around, listening closely. Lyric kept watch near the window, making sure no unwelcome guests were coming up. The whole crew had their guard up, prepared for whatever might pop off.

Jace paced the room, a slight smirk on his face as he turned to Hit. "We knew it'd come to this eventually. I ain't one to back down, and if Manny's crew and Minneapolis wants to go to war they're about to feel it he said, his voice full of confidence. "I got people who'll ride for us, you already know."

Rome nodded, a grim look in his eyes. "We gotta be surgical with this. We hit them in their weak spots, make it hurt so bad they think twice about creeping over here again. This is our blocc," he said, his voice steady, yet fierce.

"Exactly," Wild Boy chimed in, even as he shifted uncomfortably, his leg still sore. "But we ain't looking to start no unnecessary wars either. We get rid of the problem, and we handle business without extra heat."

The room fell quiet for a moment, everyone absorbing the weight of what lay ahead. Mocha glanced at her brothers, Hit and Ready, her jaw set. She didn't like this any more than they did, but family was family. If they had to take on the whole Manny's crew and their new Minneapolis backers, then so be it.

Just then, Honey's name popped up, and Red scoffed. "That chick doesn't know the first thing about loyalty. She's a wild card, and a dangerous one at that."

"Trust, we got eyes on her," Rome assured, his tone dark. "She keeps slipping up, and it won't end well."

Kaliyah walked over, setting a fresh roll of gauze on the table. "We stick together. But if anyone's bringing in trouble, we cut their ass out, no hesitation."

Shoota, leaning against the wall, nodded in agreement, his hand instinctively going to his injured arm. "Ain't no room for weak links in this chain. We roll as one, or not at all."

Enoch, quiet for most of the conversation, finally spoke up, his voice low but resonant. "I know I'm the newest here, but I'm down for whatever. Blood in, blood out. You all are my people now."

Hit gave him a nod of respect, recognizing the loyalty. They'd all been through too much to let anyone slip up or bring the crew down.

This was family. This was war. And no one—no gang, no alliance, no traitor—was about to disrupt what they'd built. The only thing left was to take it all over.

The night hung heavy with tension as HitWorld, backed by Jace and the Chicago Kings, rolled deep into Minneapolis. Wild Boy and Shoota couldn't make the trip, still healing up, but the rest of the crew was more than ready to end things tonight. Hit, Ready, Rome, Bone, and Enoch led the charge, their steps purposeful, weapons gripped tightly. Jace's crew was right there with them, side by side as if they'd been fighting together for years. Tonight wasn't just about settling scores—it was about showing Minneapolis and the world that HitWorld ran these streets.

Hit stepped out of the car, gun tucked tight in his grip. "Everybody stay sharp," he muttered, scanning the dimly lit streets. They crept through the side entrance of a rundown stash house, moving like shadows. Inside, the smell of cheap smoke and liquor hit them, voices drifting down the hallway. Hit motioned for the crew to spread out, each one taking a position.

They moved quietly down the hall until they heard it—Reek's voice, mixed with laughter. "Yeah, yeah, and Honey told us everything. Said Hit and his crew don't even see it comin'. Shoot two of

Them pussy ass niggas they took some of ours down but I feel like we got the upper hand now."

Hit tapped the door with his gun.

Reek backed up, looking around for an escape, but there was none. He was trapped, surrounded by the same crew he was just talkin' shit about. Hit took a step forward, his gun aimed steady, his gaze colder than steel.

Just then, Rome stepped forward, his expression dark.

Reek's eyes widened. "Rome, man, I swear—"

Before he could finish, Rome pulled the trigger. The gunshot echoed through the room, and Reek dropped to the ground, lifeless. Silence fell, heavy with the weight of what had just gone down.

The shootout began.

Chapter 19

As they moved in, Lyric, Red, Mocha, and Kaliyah joined them, each of them battle-ready in their own way. Mocha looked at Jace, her eyes fierce with determination. She had told him about her brothers from the start, and now he was here, proving himself worthy of the trust they'd put in him. It wasn't just business anymore; it was family.

Red had her own mission. She scanned the crowd, eyes narrowed, searching for one person in particular.

Honey's betrayal ran deep, and Red hadn't forgotten the promise she'd made to deal with that "rat" once and for all.

Honey, Juicy, and Kiki stood alongside them, traitors down to the core. Juicy's cousin, stepping up as second-in-command, sneered at the sight of HitWorld. He clearly didn't know just how outmatched he and his crew were.

"Y'all really made a mistake," Honey said with a cocky smirk, but Red didn't give her a chance to say more. She stepped forward, her voice sharp and cold.

"Shut the fuck up, rat," Red snapped. "This ends tonight."

Honey's face faltered, a flash of fear breaking through her smug look. Before she could react, Red took aim, her hands steady, and with a single shot, she made good on her word. Honey hit the ground, the echo of the shot cutting through the tense silence.

Told that bitch I was going to headshot her pussy ass red spit on her and walked off.

Kiki and Juicy's eyes went wide, scrambling back as they realized they'd backed the wrong side.

Mocha looked up at them and shot both of them bitches.

The gunfire erupted like a storm, each side firing off rounds in a brutal, merciless exchange. Hit and Ready moved with precision, covering each other, watching each other's backs as they fought through the enemy lines. Rome took his position at the front, taking down anyone who dared to step in his path. Enoch and Bone pushed forward, their relentless assault forcing the Minneapolis crew to fall back, scrambling for cover.

Jace and his crew took the flank, keeping the pressure tight. He'd had HitWorld's back from the moment Mocha told him about her brothers, and he wasn't about to back down now. He spotted Juicy's cousin, the new "leader" of the university, trying to rally the remaining fighters. Jace signaled to Rome, and in sync, they moved in. Rome fired off shots, each one hitting its mark, until Juicy's cousin fell, ending the last of the resistance.

Lyric, Kaliyah, Mocha, and Red kept watch from the back, each of them ready to jump in if needed. They held their own, unafraid, knowing they were as much a part of this fight as the men on the front lines.

As the gunfire finally faded, the blocc lay quiet, littered with the remnants of Manny's crew and Minneapolis . Hit and Ready exchanged a look, their expressions hard but satisfied. They'd taken back what was theirs, and this time, they had no intention of letting anyone take it away again.

Jace walked over to Hit, nodding in approval. "You boys move solid," he said. "Exactly what I saw from day one. This is just the beginning."

Hit nodded back, a smirk creeping onto his face. "This is our blocc now. University, Minneapolis and Saint Paul—we're takin' it all. Together."

They all stood there, catching their breath, taking in the victory that had cost them sweat, blood, and lives. Lyric, Mocha, Red, and Kaliyah joined them, relief and pride shining in their eyes. They'd fought hard for this moment, and they'd won.

As the crew regrouped, Jace leaned over to Hit, voice low but serious. "This is only the start. We got more to do, more to handle. Are you ready for what comes next?"

Hit nodded, his eyes glinting with the fire of ambition. "Always. Let's show 'em who really runs these streets."

With that, they all turned back toward the blocc, their faces set with resolve. Minneapolis was theirs now, conquered and claimed by HitWorld and the Chicago Kings. But this wasn't the end. This was just a taste of the power they could wield. And as they headed out, Hit couldn't shake the feeling that bigger battles lay ahead, that more enemies were lurking just beyond the city limits.

One thing was for sure—this was far from over. HitWorld and the Chicago Kings had only just begun, and whoever thought they could stand in their way had another thing coming.

Chapter 20

Rain misted over 3rd Street, draping the blocc in a hushed stillness as Hit stood outside Lyric's bar. The city was quieter than it had been in a long time, but it was a peace that came with scars, wounds that still ached, and memories that lingered like smoke. One by one, the crew gathered around him. Each of them carried their own pain, their own stories, yet they stood as a family, bound by the blood they'd shed and the loyalty they'd held onto.

Wild Boy stepped up first, a smirk nowhere to be found on his face. "Ain't ever gonna be the same, is it?" he muttered, more to himself than anyone. The days of laughter and wild nights had been replaced with something darker, but he didn't regret a single moment. He leaned against the wall, his gaze set, ready for whatever came next.

Shoota stood back, his hands in his pockets, eyes hard. "They tried to split us up, thinking they could break us," he said. He looked around at the crew, his voice carrying a quiet pride. "But they don't know us. Hit World ain't built to fold." His calm words masked the anger simmering beneath, a reminder that every battle they'd fought had only made them stronger.

Bone crossed his arms, his face unchanging. "This blocc is ours, and we'll hold it down until there ain't nothin' left," he said quietly. Loyalty ran through him like blood, and he'd defend his family until the end. They all knew the price they'd paid, and the toll this life was taking, but they'd made their choice. Bone wouldn't have it any other way.

Enoch appeared last, stepping out from the shadows with a steady gaze. He'd joined Hit World later, but he'd earned his place. "Ain't no real peace out here," he said, voice low but steady. His words held the weight of someone who'd seen betrayal firsthand, a reminder that they could only count on each other in this world.

Jace leaned back, his arm around Mocha, a steady presence beside her. He'd been through enough to know loyalty was rare, and he'd give everything to keep her safe. Mocha looked at her brothers, Hit and Ready, with a fierce protectiveness. She'd been through it all with them, and Jace by her side was a silent promise that he'd always have her back. Together, they stood ready for whatever the blocc would throw next.

Ready held Kaliyah close, her hand resting on his arm. They'd faced their own trials, but she was still with him, her loyalty unwavering. She looked up at him, strength and love in her gaze, a silent affirmation that they'd face the future together. Ready glanced at

Hit, a nod passing between them. Whatever came, they were all in it together.

Red leaned against the wall, arms crossed, hiding her pain behind a smirk. She glanced at Mocha, a knowing look between sisters bound by blood and loyalty. The blocc had tested her, but she'd never backed down. She was here to stay, no matter the cost.

Rome stood apart, hands in his pockets, a hard edge in his eyes. Honey's betrayal had left its mark, but he'd never been one to let someone else's choices bring him down. He looked around at the crew, his family, the people who'd always had his back. "I learned my lesson. Loyalty's a thin line out here, but y'all are solid," he said. He'd lost trust, but he'd gained clarity—Hit World was the only loyalty he needed.

Lyric stepped out, slipping her hand into Hit's. She'd seen him shoulder the weight of this life, and she was ready to face whatever came next with him. Hit looked down at her, giving her hand a gentle squeeze, knowing she'd been his anchor in the storm. Together, they'd hold onto what they'd built, no matter the cost.

Hit took a breath, looking at each of them—his brothers, his sisters, the family that had stood by him when no one else would. "Legends don't fold," he said, his voice firm. "No matter who turns their back, no matter what they throw at us. This is our blocc, and we're here to stay.

They shared a look, a silent vow passing between them all. Then, one by one, they faded into the night, each taking a piece of the blocc's legacy with them.

Hit lingered, Lyrics hand in his, looking down 3rd Street. The rain fell harder, city lights casting a glow over the quiet street. He knew the fight wasn't over,

but that didn't matter. They'd bled for this, and they'd keep fighting.

As he pulled his hood up, he whispered to himself, *"Legends never fold."*

Epilogue

Hit World: Legends Never Fold, the dust of the past settles, but the scars linger, a reminder of the lives lost and loyalties tested. Hit World has survived the war with Manny's crew and Minnepolis, coming out stronger, but not without a cost. Friends turned into enemies, and trust was a rare currency—still, the bond they shared held them together.

Ready and Kaliyah are still together, a couple shaped by the fire of survival and hardship. Kaliyah

stands by Ready's side, loyal through it all, proving that despite the chaos, love has a place even in their world. Red is with them as well, more family now than just crew, fiercely loyal to her brothers and the life they've built. She's learned to keep her circle tight, especially after seeing what betrayal can do.

Mocha, Hit, and Ready's sister, is there too, with her boyfriend Jace by her side. The trials they've endured have only brought them closer, a couple that's more like family to the entire Hit World crew.

Lyric, who once ran her bar on 3rd Street, still holds it down, making her mark in her own way, and standing as a silent strength for Hit. The city may have changed, the blocc may look different now, but the bar has become a place of loyalty, where those still standing can gather and remember.

The streets have quieted, the wars subdued, but the names of the fallen echo in every corner. This life isn't one you leave easily, but for now, they're at peace—or as close to it as Hit World will ever be. They've lived and survived, proving that legends never fold, even when the world tries to break them.

Copyright © [2024]

by [Ashley Henderson]

[Saint Paul , Mn]